For Mom and Dad

Plague of the Dead

By
Alli Rayfield

Chapter 1

I could feel my cellphone vibrating in my pocket. I knew it was Adam calling which made it less appealing to answer. He was just mad because our daughter, Jackie, was feeling ill when I left and he couldn't dump her off on the neighbors, ruining his normal Wednesday plans. I was aware of what he had been up to when I was at choir practice, even though he thought he'd been so sly about it.

I could've answered the phone though because we hadn't even begun practice, even 15 mins into our allotted time. The pianist and choir director were having a dispute over one of the arrangements. They didn't fight often but when they did it was epic and very little got done during their battles.

"You're completely out of your mind or just tone deaf," I heard Polly, our pianist, say.

"Are you really that arrogant to think you know better than me about this," Lisa shot back.

"I'm not but you are." Polly stated.

"Why can't they just get along? We're in a Church for sobbing out loud." Lauren said to me, sitting back down after visiting the bathroom. Her bright blue eyes rolling as she shook her blonde head.

I shrugged, "it's just some stupid power struggle. They have no power in their day to day lives so they've got to be in charge here."

Lauren giggled. "Thank God I wear the pants at home; I'd hate to act like that every other week."

I laughed along with Lauren.

"So Shelly, how are Adam and Jackie doing?" Lauren asked as it became obvious that we weren't going to be getting any singing done.

Almost as if on cue, I felt my phone vibrate again indicating that I had a message from Adam.

"Well, Jackie wasn't feeling very good when I left so Adam's taking care of her," I said, then added the lie, "other than that, they're good."

She nodded, "is Jackie alright?"

"Yeah," I said. "She just said she felt funny. She didn't have a fever or anything. Honestly, I think she just wanted me to stay home. She's going through a phase were she wants me to stay home with her all the time. Daddy's not good enough."

"Sara went through a phase like that. It drove me crazy. I mean no matter how much we love them, sometimes we need a break, just a little time to ourselves."

I nodded in agreement, "exactly. Excuse me a moment."

I decided to go ahead and listen to the message just in case I was wrong about Jackie faking it. I really didn't think I was though considering she had no symptoms to speak of. She just kept saying she felt funny. She said that last Wednesday too. Well last week she said she felt weird and I decided to miss practice. In ten minutes she felt better, like nothing had bothered her at all.

That's how I figured something was going on with Adam though. He went to take a quick shower because he was going to play poker with some of the guys. While he was in the shower, his phone buzzed with a text message that said "I'm so hot for you. When are you coming? And more importantly when am I?"

I was in complete shock and didn't say anything to him. I decided to wait to confront him until I knew what I was going to do about it. Finally I had come up with a plan. I was going to take Jackie with me to my sister's in Arizona but I had to wait until her roommate moved out and coming up with the money wasn't easy. A flight to Arizona from Guam wasn't exactly pocket change. My sister offered to buy the tickets so Adam wouldn't notice the charge on the credit card, which I originally declined but it became more tempting the more I stewed in my anger.

Though, the charge wouldn't cause any suspicion from Adam considering that we'd been stationed on Guam for about a year and I'd never gone that long without seeing my sister. He wouldn't think anything of me not asking him to go either since him and Cate didn't get along.

I went outside to listen to my message. After going through a bunch of messages that had to be deleted since they had been on my phone too long, I finally got to my "one new message."

"Hey, Shell, I'm taking Jackie to the ER. She's running a fever of 105.2. I don't know what happened but all of a sudden she just started burning up. You don't need to leave early; I've got it under control. Just meet me here when you're done."

Panic shot through me. Panic and shame. I'd thought Jackie had been faking it. How could I be so blind to my own child's needs? I took a few deep breaths and looked at the clock on my phone. There was more than twenty minutes to go but we hadn't practiced at all. I figured if they weren't going to be respectful of my time, I didn't need to be respectful of theirs.

When I went in Polly and Lisa hadn't let up on their stupid argument. I told Lauren that I needed to go because Adam had taken Jackie to the ER.

"Oh, dear. I hope she's all right," Lauren said sweetly.

"I'm sure she will be," I said as I got my purse and headed towards the door.

Little did I know my daughter would never be the same.

Chapter 2

My journey to the hospital was a complete blur. I couldn't remember the drive to save my life but I knew it was a miracle I didn't get stopped or in an accident. A ticket wouldn't have been the worst thing but the precious time it would've taken from me getting to my beloved Jackie would have been agony.

When I got to the hospital I ran through the front door to the main desk. I got more than a few looks of concern from the other patients waiting there.

"I'm looking for Jackie McCormick," I said before the receptionist had a chance to acknowledge me.

She was a petite girl with her long brown hair pulled back into a ponytail. She didn't look a day over sixteen and if I hadn't been on the verge of a heart attack from panic I probably would've been more curious about how she managed to get a job there.

She looked through some files and said, "They moved her to room 323 on the third floor just about fifteen minutes ago."

"Okay, thank you," I said before rushing to the elevator.

"Wait…" I heard the receptionist call behind me but I ignored her.

I pressed the button repeatedly. The doors were not opening and increasing the aggressiveness in which I hit the button wasn't making a difference. I couldn't let any more time pass than necessary so I decided to take the stairs.

I ran up the three flights taking two stairs at a time. Finally I reached the third landing completely winded. I worked out a fair amount but it seems to make no difference when it comes to climbing several flights of stairs.

Out of breath and half insane, I made my way down the hall to room 323. There was no one around. It was eerily quiet in the corridor. All of the rooms doors were closed. It looked like the corridor had been deserted.

I twisted the knob and though it was unlocked I was met with a lot of resistance from the other side. I pushed on the door but it didn't budge. I put my whole body weight against the door and pushed with every bit of strength that I had.

I managed to get the door open enough to get my body through. One of the hospital beds had been pushed up against the door. I found that very strange but it wasn't the strangest thing inside that room.

Nothing could've prepared me for what lay in front of me. There was blood everywhere. It looked like a murder scene in one of those gruesome horror movies Adam always made me watch with him that I couldn't stand.

It wasn't just blood but what were very obviously human insides. There were limbs strewn around the floor. Just beyond the hospital bed blocking the door was a man's forearm and hand. I recognized the gold wedding band on the third finger that matched my own set that I wasn't wearing and felt incredibly nauseous.

There was another person's leg in front of a chair that judging by the bloodstained white pants, must've belonged to a doctor.

That's when I finally noticed a low munching sound coming from the corner of the room and there I saw what was the cause of the destruction.

A little girl was kneeling on the floor, eating the remains of someone. I made my way around the bed and as I stepped forward, my foot landed on broken glass. It crunched loudly beneath my weight.

The little girl turned her head slowly to look at me. I knew without a doubt that this little girl had once been Jackie but she no longer looked like herself. Her skin was grey and her eyes were dead. Her teeth were a dark yellow color. She looked as if she'd been in the grave for days, maybe years, yet she was sitting there looking at me. She had muscle tissue from the person she was eating hanging from her mouth that was dripping blood on to the floor. I'd never felt so sick in my life.

"Jackie?" I whispered.

She seemed to recognize the name and the fear I probably should've felt as she began to stand and limp her decomposing body towards me never came.

As she quickened her pace, I felt frozen in place. I was too confused to make a move. She began to growl at me as she got closer but I still didn't move. I couldn't. I could only look into the dead face that once belonged to my little girl.

"Jackie?" I said again barely audible.

She reached out to grab me but when she was within inches a loud bang cried out into the room. The bullet went into the front of her head and black blood flew up into the air as she fell backwards to the floor.

"NOOOOOO!" I screamed.

Though that creature was no longer my little girl, she had once been. Maybe something could've been done to save her.

I ran to her side and knelt by her lifeless body. She smelled like decaying flesh and had blood all over the blue dress I had dressed her in that morning. I could feel my heart shatter into pieces. My head was blank from the confusion.

I put her head into my lap and stroked her hair. I was crying violently and felt my body shaking uncontrollably.

I don't know how long the doctor tried to get my attention. I didn't see him walk over to me. I didn't notice him kneel down on the other side of her body. I was lost. Too far gone in my grief.

I saw his lips moving for a minute before I finally heard his baritone voice as he said, "Mrs. McCormick."

He noticed the change in my expression as his words finally broke through whatever invisible bubble my mind had put around me.

"I'm sorry I had to do that. I'm very sorry this happened."

"You didn't have to shoot her," I whispered.

His face looked pained, "There was no other way. She was not savable."

"You don't know that," I said holding her closer to me.

He sighed, "Mrs. McCormick there was really nothing that could've been done. What happened to your daughter was something we're not able to fight."

"Well, what the hell happened to her?" I asked aggressively.

He flopped down and sighed. "That would be the question of the year."

Chapter 3

Dr. Dirk Benson introduced himself before trying to explain what had happened to my Jackie. It was some kind of plague that had been reported first in Southeast Asia, then in Africa, before outbreaks in Europe and the America's began to be reported.

"How come I haven't heard about any damn plague?" I asked confused and angry.

"It was considered something on a need to know level until just a few hours ago. No one wanted to cause a mass panic until they knew what they were dealing with and how to handle it. Well, they didn't find out anything and now more than sixty percent of the world's population is believed to be infected. That number is rapidly growing though."

"How do you get it? Is it airborne?"

"No, you have to be bitten or scratched by the infected. That's really the only thing that has been determined about it."

"And that the person who is ill is basically a walking corpse."

He nodded, "that too."

I sat there with Jackie in my arms looking at her grey face. It broke my heart to look at her eyes closed and her skin so decayed looking. She looked like she had been dead for a while and not only about ten minutes.

Dr. Benson put his hand on mine. The feel of another humans touch broke me out of my daze.

"So they're zombies basically? All that fiction about zombies come to life sort of thing?" I asked.

He pulled his hand away and rubbed the sides of his temples with both hands.

"Not exactly fiction," he stated.

"What?" I asked.

"The Zombie lore is based on a real virus. A mutated form of the black plague they believe. At least that is about the time it started happening. It seemed to disappear before it spread as rapidly as the black plague though and it wasn't considered a concern. Very few people knew about it and those that tried to tell what happened were made out to be mad or liars. It took on a life of its own of course in movies and books but it was always considered to be complete fiction by the general public. No one ever thought the disease would return, it ended so mysteriously."

"How do you know about it?" I asked.

"I've only just been privileged to the information when people started turning."

I took a deep breath not quite believing the words this doctor spoke and snapped, "So I take it vampires and aliens are real too?"

"Vampires no, the information about aliens is classified."

The look on his face suggested he was attempting a joke but I didn't find it funny.

He sighed, "Sorry. I know this is a lot to absorb. I'm struggling with it myself."

"Yeah but your daughter didn't just eat your husband and then got shot in the head by her doctor." I stated.

His brown eyes glistened in the light for a moment, "that is true."

We went back to not talking. He sat across from me but I just stared at Jackie. I felt so overwhelmed yet completely empty at the same time.

The door crashed open. I looked up and saw a nurse standing in the doorway. She was out of breath and sweaty.

"Another one turned Dr. Benson." She stated.

He let out a sigh. "I'll be there in a minute Jenny."

The nurse nodded. Her eyes were big and she looked even more scared. She left the room then.

Dr. Benson looked at me, "you need to go to the airfield."

I looked at him, "what?"

"They're evacuating people to the mainland on the airbuses. They believe it will be safer. You should go."

He got up then and walked to the door. He stopped before exiting the room entirely.

"Shelly, please. It's your best option to survive this thing." He said then added, "I'm very sorry about your loss."

He waited for me to say something but I said nothing. He left after a moment.

I heard the gunshot from down the hall. Putting down someone else's family member. Putting down another monster.

I sat there with Jackie in my arms for a while. I half expected Dr. Benson to come back but he never did.

The only family I had left was my sister, Cate, in Arizona. It made sense to get on the plane to try and get back to her. Though that would only take me to California. Something told me getting to Arizona would be extremely difficult. Yet I had nothing else but this challenge in front of me. I felt a fire begin in my belly. A fire of purpose and drive. I needed to get to Arizona from Guam to the only family I had left even though I knew then it was going to be next to, if not completely, impossible.

I kissed Jackie's forehead on the only spot not covered in thick black blood, "I'm so sorry this happened sweetie. I love you." I said.

I felt the tears in the back of my throat but I wouldn't let them fall. I couldn't grieve now. I had a mission. There would be time enough to grieve, if time for nothing else, there would be time to grieve.

I got up and walked out the door. I didn't look back at the scene of destruction in that room. There was no need. I would never forget the blood on those walls. The only thing left of my husband was his arm. Though on some level I felt he deserved it with the cheating but I still loved him. Most of all I would never forget my daughter as a zombie, the bullet going through her head and quieting her forever. If Dr. Benson had not come at that moment I would be dead because I would've never been able to take down my little girl, no matter what she had become.

I ran down the hall to the stairs. I didn't even bother with the elevator. I made my way down the stairs going way too fast. I slid down the last three, hurting my back but I got up and continued on my way.

I was running on adrenaline. I didn't stop to think. I didn't let myself think. If I let my thoughts go I knew I'd never get to the airfield.

I heard the receptionist call to me as I ran past her. I paid no mind to her. She was probably just yelling about me running through the lobby.

I made it to my car and got in. The engine gave me a bit of trouble when I tried to start it. It sounded tired and angry but finally kicked into life. I'd been meaning to take it into the shop for over a month but hadn't gotten around to it. I guess it didn't matter now.

I thought about going to the house but figured there was no time. It sounded like there was urgency in getting to that airfield.

I made my way there, though not with nearly as much urgency as I had when I was going to the hospital. I even obeyed the speed limit this time around.

I pulled into a parking lot near the hanger. I was surprised at the number of families hanging around with bags packed. Mothers were holding crying children, while fathers looked more than a bit annoyed. It was definitely no longer need to know.

I saw one of our friends, Richard, standing outside with a clipboard. It looked as though he was making some kind of announcement to the crowd.

I got out of my car and walked over to Richard; he saw me and smiled. "Shelly! Adam got the message then?" he asked, giving me a brief hug. "Where are Jackie and Adam?"

"What message?" I asked.

"That you guys are to be on the second plane out. The evacuation plan. People are lining up in hopes that families don't show up. The first plane is leaving in about ten minutes; yours should be leaving in about an hour."

I was beyond confused at this point and I guess it could be read written all over my face.

"You do know what's going on right?" Richard asked.

"Only that my daughter turned into some kind of undead flesh eating thing and killed my husband and a couple doctors. The doctor gave me an idea of what was going on but I don't really get how this is happening so fast."

"I'm so sorry Shelly, I can't believe that happened." Richard said, sorrow filling his eyes. Adam was one of his dearest friends.

He blinked back a few tears and cleared his throat. "They made the official announcement of what's going on around six o'clock, right before all the TV and internet service went down."

The announcement happened when I was at choir practice. Adam missed it because he had taken Jackie to the hospital. In less than an hour of that important announcement we both missed, our world crashed down.

Then I realized just what he had said, "TV and internet went down?"

"Everything's down. We lost communication with the base in D.C. who was in charge of orders. When we tried to contact other bases, we couldn't get a hold of them. We hoped it was a glitch of some type because we were able to stay in contact with the Air Force bases in Japan and Hawaii. We lost contact with them just a little while ago."

I couldn't believe what I was hearing. How could something this bad be happening so fast? And whose best interest was it to be so quiet about it for so long? If they had given us a chance to protect ourselves would things maybe have turned out differently? There was no way of knowing. Now it was a fight for survival. Enter in the plague of the dead.

Chapter 4

Richard showed me into the hanger. There were also several families in there, though they seemed slightly more at ease than the ones outside. I guess like me it made them feel better to be doing something or feel like they were getting somewhere.

Richard gave me a hug before returning to his post. I sat down and pulled out my cell phone. The only possession I had other than my car keys, which didn't seem necessary anymore but I kept them on me.

I hit my sister's name on the screen and hit the call button, hoping service would still work. Thankfully the phone was ringing on the other end. I held my breath until she answered.

"Hello," she said.

"Cate," I said.

"Shelly, thank God. I wasn't sure if you were alright."

"Well, I'm alive but I wouldn't say I was alright."

"Why?"

"Jackie and Adam..." I couldn't get past their names, it was too much. I felt my body go numb. The crushing weight of loss was taking over.

"Shelly, I'm so sorry. I don't even know where to begin with this mess. How are you going to get home? Can you? They've grounded all commercial flights."

"Yeah, I should be boarding a military airbus in about an hour but they're taking us to an Air Force base in California."

She let out a sigh of relief, "that's better still. You won't be an ocean away."

I heard static start to cut in; I knew the phone service would not allow this conversation to last much longer.

"Listen, no matter what happens, just remember I love you."

"I love you t..."

With that, the phone went dead. Complete silence met me at the other end. Somehow I couldn't fight the feeling that that was the last conversation I would have with my sister. I almost lost all my sanity right then and there. I knew that I couldn't give up hope. Maybe I'd be able to see her again.

The time passed by so slowly. Children were getting antsy, tired and upset. Mothers were becoming frustrated and the fathers angry. It reminded me of when we had flown to Guam the year prior. It was a long flight and we were stuck at LAX for a seven hour layover due to engine trouble. Jackie was tired and fussy. Adam and I were fighting. Then Jackie climbed up in my lap and laid her head down. She then said "I love you Mommy." With that little phrase everything felt so much better. Adam was still acting like a jerk as Jackie had begun to fall asleep but I sat there and ran my fingers through her curly brown hair.

Now I sat here watching these families fighting and getting aggravated with each other, none of them realizing how lucky they were to still have each other. At that moment I was happy I didn't have a gun because my sorrow was border lined with rage and I could've shot them all for taking each other for granted.

They had given everyone a muffin and a bottle of water. It was a nice gesture but it didn't calm anyone's nerves. It didn't answer the growing questions. More than an hour had gone by and no one had said anything about boarding the airbus.

I saw Richard walking towards me. I had a sinking feeling in my stomach the closer he got. He was pale and looked stressed.

"You need to go home." He said to me quietly.

"What?" I asked confused.

"Go home, pack a bag and some food just in case and go to the Navy Base."

"Why?"

"The first airbus is gone. It crashed in the ocean. Someone on board was infected and turned."

I felt my whole body go cold. My heart had dropped somewhere into my stomach. It was like I was in an unending nightmare.

"The Navy is still sending out ships but we're grounding all the flights. You still have a chance to get out of here. Shelly it's the only shot you've got. I'm sorry, but you need to go. They're going to make the announcement in about ten minutes. Get out of here before the shit storm starts. They're going to put the base on lockdown at 2300 hours. You've got less than two hours to get out of here."

"Maybe it would be better to stay," I said. Since they were going to put the base on lockdown, maybe it would be the safest bet. It split me in two to think that I would never see my sister again but I had a bad feeling about leaving even though the Navy base was only 30 miles away.

He sighed, "No Shelly, I think the only hope would be to get off the island. It's only a matter of time before everyone here is infected. If you can leave, do it."

I nodded in understanding and gave him a hug.

"Okay. Thank you. Try to stay alive."

He gave a weak smile, "you too."

Chapter 5

I didn't remember leaving the hanger or the drive to my house. It was all a blank, like I had been drinking all night.

I walked into the duplex that I lived in with my family for the past year. The little space we had called home. I hit the light switch as I walked in. The lights worked but they were flickering. The backup generator for typhoons must have kicked in. It made me feel uneasy, like I was walking into a horror movie or a trap.

I realized walking into my home just how exhausted I was. It wasn't just physically being tired, I was emotionally drained. I felt tired in every bone in my body; each muscle was lined with fatigue. All I wanted was to sleep, maybe even sleep forever. I knew if I slept I would be stuck. Though I wasn't convinced that was such a bad idea.

I thought Richard was wrong. He was over reacting to the situation. There was no way that the whole island would be infected. It just didn't seem possible. If Dr. Benson was correct and this was a disease that had existed before, it would certainly phase out again. Besides it managed to disappear in a time that they did not have the science and medical advances we were privileged to now. I just didn't believe that our world was down and out yet. Despite everything I had seen in less than six hours a part of me was hopeful that things would come together in the end. Besides, if everyone would get infected on the island who's to say that the whole world wouldn't be infected by the time a ship made it too the coast of California.

I made my way to the master bedroom that I shared with Adam. I noticed an odd smell as I made my way down the hall. It smelled like something had crawled in the walls and died. I ignored it and continued into the bedroom.

I grabbed a backpack Adam had used for camping. I packed a few clothes and an extra pair of tennis shoes. I opened the drawer to our nightstand. I grabbed Adam's .45 and the holster lying next to it. I loaded the clip into it and secured the holster with the gun around my waist.

I got the extra bullets, flashlight, and a first-aid kit from the closet at the end of the hall. I put a small photo album with my favorite photos of my family in the bag as well. I knew it was excessive but I felt I needed to have those photos with me.

I was about to go to the kitchen to get some more supplies when I heard a thumping coming from Jackie's room. The door was closed which was unusual. I looked at the door for a moment. The thumping began to get louder as I stood there.

I heard a faint growling as well on the other side of the door. It was a low slow growl, unlike any animal I had ever heard before.

The smell I had ignored upon entering the hall was stronger now. I knew it was coming from in there. I knew what it was. Jackie had reeked of that smell. I just didn't understand what one was doing in my house.

I put down the backpack. I readied the gun and cautiously opened the bedroom door. I was not prepared for the monster to come at me as fast as it did. The creature lunged at me as soon as I opened the door. It had managed to knock the gun from my hand and pushed me up against the wall.

It hadn't managed to scratch or bite me yet. I pushed on the zombie's neck to keep the rotting teeth in its mouth from sinking into my flesh.

It had once been a her and her skin was the same greyish color that Jackie's had been. The eyes in her head were lifeless. She smelled of death. She kept chomping her teeth, trying to get a piece of me in reach.

I lifted my leg and hit her with my knee as hard as I could. It was an awkward angle but I managed to strike a blow in her abdomen.

It worked. I was able to push her into the opposite wall and get out of her death grasp. It didn't buy me much time.

I ran into the kitchen with her right on my tail. I knocked over the ironing board that had been left in the kitchen. It served a great purpose of buying me time but only a few more seconds as the zombie tried to maneuver around it. I grabbed my biggest knife from the set sitting on the counter.

I prepared myself as she came at me. I blocked her with my left hand and she moved her head forward. I stabbed her right between her lifeless eyes. She stopped chomping at me and fell to the floor.

I finally realized who the zombie was. I was in too much of a panic to really pay attention to the facial features of this creature. I should've known the whole time who it was but I never could've imagined Adam would be that low.

The decaying lifeless zombie that lay on the floor with thinning blond hair was once Jennifer Dawson. The woman I had seen the text from only a week ago. The blood in my body began to boil.

I pulled the knife out of her skull and stabbed her again and again. I don't know how many times I drove the sharp edge of that knife into her head, my anger had over taken my body, driving me into a rage and pointless over kill of this zombie.

By the time I was done, her head and face were destroyed. Zombie brains and black blood were all over the kitchen floor and on my hands and clothes. I sat down on the floor leaning against the counter.

I began to cry then. The tears I had fought came pouring out me. I was crying so violently it hurt my entire body. My grief and sorrow collided with the hurt and rage I'd been fighting for the past week causing me to completely lose control.

When the tears stopped coming, I looked at Jennifer. I let out a sigh "my own house, you stupid bitch," I said before kicking her lifeless undead body.

Chapter 6

I managed to pull myself together. There wasn't a lot of time left to leave if I was going to and I still hadn't got all my stuff together. If I had had any desire to stay it was gone. Seeing your husband's undead mistress will have that effect on a person.

I stepped over Jennifer's body and made my way out of the kitchen. I walked down the hallway feeling completely out of place, like I was in a movie or dreaming. When I made it back to the bedroom I realized that the knife was still in my hand.

The blade was covered in brain matter and black blood. I picked up a towel that Adam had left on the door knob and wiped off the blade. I set the knife on the bed deciding to take it with me. It had come in so handy, I felt it might bode well to take it along.

I changed into some clean clothes. I really didn't have time to shower but I desired one more than I ever have in my life. I used a wash cloth to wipe off the blood from my face and arms. It was disgusting.

In addition to the kitchen knife, I grabbed one of Adam's hunting knives as well. I placed them in the front pocket of the backpack. I found the .45 on the floor by the linen closet from when it was knocked out of my hand. I picked it up and placed it back in the holster.

I paused by Jackie's room feeling the sorrow fill up in my heart. I walked in to her room and turned on the light. I took in all her things for one last time. Her Disney Princess bedspread, her toys and books. She had just begun to learn how to read and was so excited every time she learned a new word and when she was able to read a whole sentence without asking what any of the words were. Her coloring books were strewn about all over the floor.

I felt the tears sting behind my eyes and though I didn't give in to them, I didn't actively fight them either.

I saw her favorite stuffed animal sitting at the foot of her bed. It was a white duck she called Chinny. I picked it up and stuffed it into my bag.

I turned to exit, not bothering to cut the light out. I wanted to leave it on for Jackie. There would always be a light on for my little girl though she was never going to come home.

I went back into the kitchen half expecting the zombie to be back on her feet, to attack me and take me out of my miserable life. She didn't. She just laid there useless and destroyed.

I made my way past the fridge to get to the cabinet where we kept our typhoon supplies. I had to push the dead zombie out of my way to get to the food supply. It was only difficult due to the fact I was exhausted and my body wanted to give out any second.

I decided not to take too many canned foods. I mostly just stuck to protein bars and a couple of the astronaut meals that we had in there. I didn't take very much figuring I wouldn't need a lot. It only took maybe an hour to get to the Navy base but I wanted to have something so I wouldn't have to depend on the supplies on the ship. Lastly I grabbed a gallon of water and I was on my way.

I went outside, not bothering to lock the door behind me. People could take whatever they wanted, I would never be back. The thought made me kind of sad but of all the things I had lost that night, my material possessions were not important.

It was extremely quiet out and there were no lights anywhere. It made me feel uneasy as I made my way to my car. I put my things in the back seat and climbed into the driver's seat. I started the car without any trouble which made me let out a sigh of relief. I saw that it was 10:43 on the clock. I had seventeen minutes to get off the base before they initiated lockdown.

There was no one on the road, which I found strange but I made it to the gate very fast. The guards let me go with a tip of their hat. I felt a little odd all of a sudden. I hadn't thought it through how silly my plan might actually be but I rolled with it. I kept telling myself, "What else do I have?"

What did I have? Nothing at all. The only thing that I had left was a crazy will to survive and I needed this mission even if it was the dumbest thing I ever did. I was probably going to die anyway, it'd be better to die fighting for something no matter how stupid it was than to sit around my house all alone waiting for death to come bite me in the throat.

I got on to the main road and knew immediately I was in trouble. I couldn't leave the lights on because there were two zombies ahead of me and the brightness caught their attention. I turned off the lights as quickly as I could but then I couldn't see anything. The world was swallowed in darkness.

It hadn't crossed my mind about driving at night with these monsters on the roads. I pulled over to the side. I looked at the clock, it was 11:10. It was too late to go back now.

I made sure the doors were locked and put the sunshade in the windshield in hopes of concealing myself from the monsters outside. I climbed over the center console and sat on the floor in between the seats.

There was a blanket I left in the car for Jackie. I wrapped it around my body. Despite the tropical weather, I was shaking.

I heard the noises of the undead rustling in the jungle beyond my car. I took a deep breath. The fear would not change that I was stuck until the sun made an appearance. It also wouldn't change the fact that in less than eight hours I had lost everything except the air coming into my lungs. Honestly that wasn't a blessing because breathing was feeling more like dying. Every breath was a fight to take in. I felt like a sumo wrestler was sitting on my chest.

I laid my head against the backseat. The tears came easily and without a single thought. They ran down my check. I didn't wipe them away; they just ran together and began to dry on my face.

I thought of Jackie's angelic face. I would give anything to see that beautiful face again. With that thought, my fear seemed to subside. At least if those undead creatures got me, I would be with Jackie again. Thinking about Jackie I closed my eyes and I fell asleep.

Chapter 7

I ran as fast as I could through the jungle, yet the slow moving zombies were gaining on me. There were at least a dozen of them and they seemed to be working together to get me. Assisting each other in obtaining some lunch. My heart was racing and I was completely out of breath.

I looked behind me to see how far they were behind me and I felt my foot catch on something. I fell hard to the earth; the entirety of my right side was in extreme pain. I couldn't move. They were closing in on me. Growling, grabbing, and scratching at me. There was nothing I could do but scream as the yellow teeth of a young male zombie closed in on the soft flesh of my neck...

I woke up completely confused. The dream had seemed so real. I even felt the pain in my right side and in my neck, which after a few conscious moments I realized had to do with the cramped quarters I had fallen asleep in.

The sun was shining in through the windows. With the blanket still on me, I was sweating profusely. I put the blanket in my backpack to have just in case.

My mouth was so dry; I took a long refreshing sip of water. I didn't drink as much as I wanted though. I was trying to conserve my rations. Unable to brush my teeth, I popped a piece of gum in my mouth.

There was a pack of wipes I kept in the car for Jackie when she had snacks in the car. I used one to wash my face and rinsed under my arms with it in an attempt not to feel completely disgusting. I added the wipes to my backpack.

I ran a brush threw my hair and put it up in a ponytail. I was trying to busy myself and feel normal. I didn't want thoughts of the day before to creep into my psyche. Not yet. With any luck, I'd be at the Navy base in about an hour's time.

I climbed over the center console back into the driver's seat. It took a moment to find what I had done with my keys and after ten minutes of searching, I found them wedged between the passenger side seat and the center console.

I put the keys in the ignition and turned, the engine however, did not. It made that sad little noise it had made all month but this time it didn't kick into life after its complaining. I let go of the key and decided to wait a moment.

I looked out into the distance. About a hundred yards away sat a zombie eating on some kind of animal. I felt uneasy and just wanted nothing more than to get a move on. I turned the key again but nothing.

I kept at it but all I got was a choking noise before she stopped giving me anything at all. It was dead and gone. Just another addition to the list of things I had lost in less than 24 hours.

I tried not to panic but I felt like I was being crushed. That I couldn't breathe. What was I going to do? It would maybe take a day or two to walk to the base if I made good time but I didn't think I could do it. How would I survive that journey with all these monsters that wanted to eat me?

"Now is the time to be strong," I whispered to myself.

I took a deep breath and opened the door. I got out of the car as quietly as I could. The zombie down the road never looked up from her meal as I got my bag and closed the door.

I put my jug of water on the hood while I adjusted the backpack so the weight would distribute evenly since it was such a far walk. I was messing with the bag and didn't notice anything unusual. Not until I felt something pull on my bag.

I turned to see another female zombie growling and grabbing at me. I reached for the gun at my hip only to discover it wasn't there. I looked into the car to see that it was sitting on the backseat. The knives were located in the bag.

I quickly ran to the other side of the car. The zombie chased after me. I tried to get into the car but I didn't have the time. The zombie was very close to grabbing me when I put my hand on the handle of the backdoor. I ran again with no idea what to do next. If I didn't have time to get into the car to grab the gun, I didn't have time to grab the knives. I couldn't believe my lack of planning. I was not at all prepared for this and I should've been. I knew what the stakes were getting out of car and yet I let myself be blindsided. It was like I had some kind of subconscious death wish.

Gaining my senses a little bit I realized a way to outsmart the zombie. I should be able to outsmart it; after all, I was the one still alive.

I went around one more time and stopped when I got to the back door on the passenger side. I unhitched the door but didn't open it all the way. When the zombie got close enough I opened the door quick.

The zombie had no sense or reflexes really and ran right into the door as I had hoped she would. She fell backwards and thumped hard on the ground. Her growls became louder and more annoyed. I knew I didn't have long before she managed to roll over and either crawl or stand and walk after me.

I grabbed the gun and clip off the seat. I put the clip into the gun quickly. When I took my head out of the back of the car, there was no growling. The zombie was making no noise at all. I looked up and saw the reason why.

A woman with black as night hair, almost black eyes, and beautiful dark skin was standing about 6 feet away from me by the head of the zombie. She had put a spear through the zombies head.

"You looked like you could've used some help," she said as she took the spear out of the zombies head.

"A bit yeah," I said back.

"Phoebe," she said and outstretched her hand.

I took her hand and shook it, "Shelly."

"Are you all alone?"

"Yeah, I was headed to the navy base when my car broke down. I was going to try to make it on foot."

"Well, my group is headed to a beach over that way. Would you want to join us?"

I was surprised by her offer and a little scared to take her up on it. After all, I didn't know these people; they could be cannibals or something crazy like that. On the other hand if I stayed on my own, I'd probably end up as zombie food. I figured I'd take my chances on the people who weren't guaranteed to want to eat me.

"If you think it wouldn't be a problem?"

"No problem at all, the more the merrier."

I put the gun in my holster and grabbed my things. I followed behind Phoebe as she led the way to where her group had set up camp. She explained that her boyfriend and a few friends had decided it might be best to go to the other end of the island to this beach where there were caves to help keep them safe. She said she had needed a few minutes to herself and that's why she was away from her group, out on the road.

I heard the laughter of a man as we approached the camp. It was maybe ten feet off the main road hidden well in the jungle area.

As we approached the camp, one of the guys asked, "Find anything good?"

"Just this," Phoebe replied pointing to me. "This is Shelly. She's on her way to the Navy base and her car broke down so I thought she could join us."

"Cool, someone who's alive." Said a dark skinned man. He was positively gorgeous with smooth black hair and light brown eyes that had flakes of green in them. "I'm Robert," he said and shook my hand.

"Nice to meet you," I said.

"Daniel," said the guy who had spoken first. He was more rugged than the others. He was tanned from spending a lot of time in the sun. He had messy brown hair, a short but unkempt beard and big muscles. He was definitely one to have in the group; he could knock a zombie out easily. Also, I was strongly attracted to him. I couldn't remember the last time I'd felt such strong lust for a man on first sight. It was a nice distraction from the pain of my broken heart like a celebrity or teen crush.

The other guy in the group didn't say anything. He just continued to eat his food.

The girl next to him, who was a tiny wisp of a thing with long brown hair and a friendly face smiled and said, "I'm Jamie, this is Freddie." She nudged the gloomy man next to her.

He still said nothing. I got the impression he was not happy with my presence. I didn't really care.

"Have some breakfast, Robert wasted some of the eggs and made too much," Phoebe said.

"Habit," Robert said. "Besides the Lord told me we'd have another one arriving."

"Did he now? Is that why you made enough for about 5 more people?"

"Well he didn't say how hungry she would be," he said.

I laughed and took the plate he had made me as he spoke.

"We don't have time to wait for her to eat," Freddie said matter of factly.

I felt my patience snap in two. After everything I'd been through in less than 24 hours, I was not about to put up with this asshole.

"I'm sure I'll be finished by the time you take down the tents and get all your things packed. Plus it seems you need some extra time to remove that stick that's lodged up your ass."

Everyone but Freddie laughed. He glared at Jamie and she immediately stopped laughing. I was tempted to take the .45 and shoot him.

"I like her," Phoebe said.

"No one talks to me like that," Freddie said ignoring Phoebes comment.

"Come on Freddie, you're being a jerk" said Robert. Phoebe and Daniel nodded in agreement.

"I don't want this bitch in our group," he snapped.

"You seem to be the only one who feels that way," Daniel said. "She has her own gun; I think she could prove to be useful."

"I don't want her here!"

"Nobody asked what you wanted." Daniel replied.

Phoebe smiled, "Sounds like it's settled to me."

Chapter 8

Freddie didn't respond to Phoebe. Instead he just sulked and fussed at Jamie, who I realized now was his girlfriend, about their tent. After fussing at her he began to help Daniel with getting things put away.

I sat down and began to eat the eggs that Robert had made. Robert was next to me, cleaning up the remaining remnants of their meal.

The eggs were delicious. I told Robert that I thought so.

"Thanks," he said. "I used to be a chef."

"You still are obviously," I said.

He smiled big, "thank you. I guess it does take some skill to make something good on just a fire in the ground and not a stove."

"Yeah and you did a great job. I'm a right awful cook so this is quite a treat. Where'd you get the eggs?"

"There were some wild chickens a few yards back and there were a bunch of eggs. I grabbed some as we walked up. Figured it be a nice breakfast. Nice to feel normal for a moment before the chaos of the day starts."

"Yeah, true. It's just too bad there's no bacon. Now that's a complete breakfast."

He laughed, "That's true. I make the best bacon."

"I wouldn't doubt it. So how do you all know each other?" I asked.

"Well, Phoebe's my girlfriend; we've been dating for about five years now. Daniel's been a good friend since we were teens; he stayed here after their parents moved back to the states after being stationed here. Jamie's his baby sister, she moved back here after graduating high school. She and Freddie have been together for a little over a year now unfortunately."

"So, he's always like that then? Not some effect from the stress of being attacked by the undead?"

He laughed, "No, he's always been this way to an extent. Daniel can't stand the guy, thinks he's no good for his sister, which is partly the truth. But you can't always make people see that."

"No, you can't," I agreed remembering all too well how a lot of my friends thought Adam wasn't good enough for me. Even Cate mentioned it once or twice. I never listened though, thinking my heart knew best. The logic turned out to be wrong on my part. There was no point in dwelling on it now, he was dead and I probably wouldn't be far behind.

"So what are you doing out here?" he asked.

"I was trying to get to the Navy base. One of my friends said they would have ships taking people out. I was hoping to get to Arizona to my sister, though it is a long shot."

"They weren't sending out any planes?"

"They were. The one they sent crashed because one of the passengers had the virus and turned during the flight. They decided not to take the risk of sending out any more flights."

He nodded, "are they going to continue sending out ships then?"

"I don't know. Believe me; I know how stupid it is to be doing this."

"Not stupid, we all got to do what we feel is right. There's no guide map to this situation, we're all just going along blind."

I smiled, "yeah, I guess you're right."

"Well, it's good to have you along. Even if it's just for a little while."

Robert began to pack up all the plates and the camp cooking gear that he had out.

I worked on finishing my eggs when Jamie sat down next to me.

"Hi," she said with a little smile. "I just wanted to say how sorry I am about Freddie. He doesn't like things changing what he had set up in his mind. He's very set in his ways. I'm sure he'll warm once he gets to know you."

"Thanks, but you don't need to be sorry. You did nothing wrong but I appreciate your kind words."

She smiled. "Are you good with that?" she asked pointing to the .45 in my holster.

"I'm a fair shot. Not great but I hit what I'm aiming for eighty percent of the time."

"Cool, I can't use a gun for shit. I'm just here for decoration anyway. That's what Freddie always says. You're going to make it through this," she stated.

"Well, I'm in your group so I guess that means you're going to make it too."

She shook her head, "no, I don't count on it. I just hope whatever happens to me is quick. Daniel is good at this, he'll make it but I don't have my hopes up too high." She stood up then, "It's good to have you." She walked over to get her stuff put away.

What she said left me feeling raw in the pit of my stomach. It was sad to think someone so young had themselves marked for death. She didn't even hope to make it. I was trying to accept that death was highly likely but I didn't want to just give into it either. She actually had something to live for, while I was just alone in the dark.

I finished my food though it was hard to enjoy after talking to Jamie. I know she didn't mean it that way. I wanted to punch Freddie for telling her she was just decoration. I got the feeling that wasn't something new he had told her. He wanted her to feel useless so she wouldn't think she could take care of herself. And if you hear something often enough, you tend to believe it after a while.

After I finished, I helped Robert get stuff put away. I'd been there about an hour and half when everyone was ready to go.

Daniel was the leader of the group it seemed. Everyone followed him. Phoebe and Robert walked hand in hand behind him, and Jamie and Freddie were third in line though not nearly as affectionate. I took up the rear which I wasn't comfortable with but I didn't say anything. I didn't want to complain.

After the zombie coming up behind me at the car, I was terrified of one managing to sneak up behind me again. I kept looking behind me every few seconds, checking to see if I was about to become a zombie's lunch but nothing was ever there.

In fact, we came across nothing at the start that would be a threat. It was almost peaceful. Almost because the longer we didn't come across something, the more concerned I got. The last twenty-four hours had kicked peaceful to the curb, so where were the undead creatures that wanted to tear us each apart and eat us as bar-b-que? Why would they shut down the base if there wasn't an immediate threat?

My mind wouldn't stop racing. I was losing it. Too much had happened and I was beginning to be overcome by fear. No one was really talking in the group so that made it worse. I was surrounded by silence except for the sound of my own thoughts that would not leave me be.

Chapter 9

The heat was beginning to get overbearing. It was only in the seventies but it was a tropical island and the humidity was a nightmare. I drank sips of water periodically, careful not to drink too much. I just drank enough not to be overcome by dehydration but I didn't want to use all of it because I didn't know how easy it would be to find more if it came down to it. It was terrible to be surrounded by water, trapped by it if I was honest, but all that water couldn't save you if you needed it.

Though it would be just as bad if not worse in the desert. Which made me think about Cate. I slipped my phone out of my pocket to see if it came back to life. It hadn't. I had no bars available. Even if towers were somehow working again, it wouldn't do any good. I had half my battery left. It would be gone by the end of the night and there was no way for me to charge it now that my car was also dead.

No way to contact Cate, I slipped my phone back into my pocket. I had no way of knowing if she was alright. If she had survived as long as I had. I didn't know what was worse. I'd lost Jackie and Adam but I knew what had happened to them. I knew they were gone; I had no way of knowing about Cate. I could only imagine what fate she was met by. I prayed she was still alive but I could not know for sure.

Even if I was able to get on a ship and make it to California and then somehow be able to get a car to get to Arizona, how would I find her? There was no way she would stay home. It seemed no one had stayed home. It didn't feel safe too. But there was maybe a slight chance she had. She could, I guess. Though I wouldn't bank on it.

I tried to not think about it anymore so I paid more attention to my surroundings. Jamie was feeling the heat bad.

She lost a bit of color in her face and looked extremely tired. Phoebe and Robert seemed to be doing alright but Phoebe was turning a very bright red color. Freddie was wasting water, drinking it and then pouring it on his face. Jamie told him to stop and he snapped at her.

The only one who seemed to be doing alright was Daniel. I got the feeling he hiked and spent much more time outdoors than the rest of us.

"Does anybody need a break?" he asked.

"Yes," said several people at once.

We came to a halt. I sat down and was joined by Phoebe and Robert.

"How you holding up?" she asked.

"Alright, you?" I said.

"Been better," she smiled and drank some water.

"Where is our daily rain? It can come at any time now!" Jamie stated.

"Stop complaining Jamie," Freddie snapped.

"Well, not all of us have been wasting water pouring it on our faces like you so why don't you give her a break?" I said.

"Listen you lit..." he began.

"You've been pouring water on your face?" Daniel asked.

'Yeah, a little, to stay cool."

Daniel ripped the gallon of water out of Freddie's hand. Freddie was so taken by surprise; he didn't try to get it back.

"Hey," was all he managed to say.

"You're not going to waste water Freddie. We need it to drink if we hope to stay alive."

"Well we wouldn't need it if we had just stayed home instead of going on this stupid trip to nowhere."

Daniel glared at him, "It wasn't safe at home, besides I don't recall anyone saying your ass had to tag along. You can go back anytime you damn well please. Believe me you'd be doing everyone a favor."

"Daniel," Jamie said but it wasn't very loud.

Daniel let out a sigh and turned, walking about ten feet before leaning against a tree.

"I don't need you to fight my battles Jamie; I can handle your stupid brother."

I snapped, "listen shithead, she was just trying to defend you which you don't even deserve so instead of being such a jerk about it be appreciative that she actually cares about you. I mean honestly Daniel could probably kick your ass in his sleep."

I heard Daniel laugh but he didn't turn around.

"You have a lot of opinions for someone who just joined our group about three hours ago," Freddie barked.

"And you have a lot of opinions for someone without a brain."

Phoebe laughed. Freddie chewed the inside of his cheek but said nothing. He turned and walked to the opposite direction of Daniel. Jamie followed him.

"Well, that's fun then." I said and stood up.

I walked over towards Daniel.

"You're not really scared of anything are you?" he asked seeming somewhat amused.

"There's nothing scary about Freddie. Besides, after your daughter almost rips off your face, very little is scary anymore." I didn't mean to say it. I didn't really want to discuss Jackie with these people. I didn't want Freddie to have a reason as to why I might be incapable of handling myself.

"What?" Daniel asked, looking concerned.

"Um," I began, feeling unable to back out of it now, "My kid, Jackie, she turned. She killed my husband and tried to kill me and that's why I'm here."

"I'm sorry," he said.

"Me too. Don't tell anyone please. I don't know why I told you. I really don't want to make it a big deal."

"It is a big deal."

"Yeah, but it's my big deal. No one else needs to know about it."

He nodded, "They won't think you're weak because you lost your family."

I felt unnerved then, like he could see through me and I didn't like it at all.

"I know but…."

"It's okay; I won't say anything to anyone. If you need to talk though, I'll listen."

I nodded, "thanks."

"We ready yet?" Phoebe asked. "If I sit here to long, I'm going to fall asleep."

"Yeah, we should head on." Daniel agreed. He patted me on the shoulder as he walked by.

I let out a sigh, feeling strange. Life didn't feel like life anymore. I felt like I had fallen into some kind of strange dream.

I turned and joined them as we continued onward.

Chapter 10

I didn't want to be in the back alone anymore, I felt like walking food back there. So I stayed in the front with Daniel.

Daniel wasn't a man of many words but he did keep a conversation going with me about growing up and how he was worried about his and Jamie's mom and dad in Ohio. He hadn't been able to get a hold of them before his cellphone lost reception. It was nice not to be stuck in my own head even if the talk wasn't really any less grim. I guess I didn't feel alone in my despair anymore.

My parents died a few years back. My mom had inoperable cancer and only a few months later my dad passed away. His heart was so broken after mom's death that it seemed to just stop. I missed them every day and still found myself about to dial my mom's number when I wanted to tell her something funny or something cute Jackie did. I'd wanted nothing more than to talk to her last week when I found out about Adam's infidelity to get her advice and prospective on the subject. The heart doesn't accept loss easily.

As much as I missed them though this was the first time since their death I was relieved they were gone. Hearing Daniel talk about his worry for his parents, I was relieved they didn't see this awful turn the world had taken. My relief I'll admit was also selfish. I don't think I could've survived with two more people I loved out there and not knowing what fate they might meet. It was hard enough just knowing Cate was out there somewhere alive, dead, or eating on other people's flesh.

In reality though, if my parents had been alive, I'd probably would've left Guam after I found out about Adam to stay with them. I had intended to go to my sister's but part of the reason I had waited was until after her roommate moved out next week since there was no room for Jackie and me until then. I would've been with my family now and Jackie would still be alive had that been the case. I tried not to let my mind dwell on what might've been, I needed to focus on staying alive.

Daniel got onto the subject of how the government covered this up until it was too late and if they would've told us sooner we might've had more of a chance. I was confused by the sudden change of subject and didn't really follow his train of thought having gone so deep into my own mind for a moment.

"They were trying to stop it. They didn't want a panic from what I heard." I said, since that was what Dr. Benson had told me.

"Maybe, but it seems to me that they probably knew early on there was no way of stopping this from spreading. They could've given us time to prepare ourselves."

I nodded. "True."

"They did cover it up. Didn't you hear about that reporter?" he asked.

"What reporter?"

"There was this reporter in Boston or New York who released a story about incidences with the undead and got fired. The story was mocked and called complete trash and only a few weeks later it turned out to be true."

I did vaguely remember hearing something about a reporter who got fired over an article about some kind of plague outbreak. It was one of those stories that you hear about and think is completely ridiculous and dismiss immediately. Turns out it was one not to be ignored.

"I thought it was ludicrous," I said.

Daniel gave off a bit of a laugh, "me too. Thought she must have been crazy, turns out she was right."

We stopped for a quick bite however it was really more to do with the fact Jamie wasn't feeling well. She didn't eat anything, just drank some water. I wasn't hungry either. I was so hot I felt like I wouldn't be able to hold much down. Even breakfast felt like it was going to make a comeback sometime soon.

We weren't making the greatest time which worried me. I didn't know how long they would still be running the ships out of the Navy base, how many they had or even if they hadn't already stopped. I felt like I was on an invisible time table and no idea of how long it actually lasted. It was like trying to run against an unseen hour glass and it was driving me crazy. I couldn't go on by myself and I didn't want to make these people who were generous enough to invite me into their group feel rushed but at the same time I wished we'd get a move on. The heat wasn't making it easy though.

After what felt like an eternity, we got on our way. It wasn't a long walk before we came across the devastation. The main road was littered with cars that were abandoned. To the naked eye it might look like a huge traffic jam but it was more than that.

We slowly made our way through the mass of cars. It was an unpleasant sight. Almost like witnessing a deadly accident. A lot of the cars had blood on the seats. I even noticed the sight of torn muscle tissue in one of them. It felt like a biology class for the demented that wouldn't end. I felt my stomach drop. A feeling of dread like I'd never known washed over me.

In one of the cars, a zombie sat in the front seat, scratching at the window. It seemed to be trapped by the seatbelt still being buckled. There was torn flesh visible on the zombie's neck. Where it had come across the other zombie that was responsible was a mystery.

"Come on," Daniel said for all of us stopped to look at the zombie struggling to get us from the car.

Yet, there seemed to be no other zombies around. That's what made me nervous. People wouldn't just abandon their cars for one zombie stuck in the driver seat of a car. Most people probably wouldn't even notice that zombie.

No, something happened. Something big must've transpired. Why else would everyone leave? But what could've happened that would make so many people just take off. There weren't a lot of places to go. We were on a tiny island. As far as I knew, no safe haven had been set up for the citizens on Guam, if there were any at all in the world. So where would they go? Only extreme fear would make them take off like that, I was sure of it. I felt extremely uneasy.

There was also an odor that was thick and heavy in the air. It was getting stronger too, the further into the traffic we got. I knew the smell. I knew it when I walked into the hospital room where Jackie was, the smell that reeked from Julie's every dying pore. This was much stronger than either of those had been. The smell of death. The stench of decaying flesh hung heavy in the tropical heat, multiplied by tens, perhaps even more.

Chapter 11

"Something's not right," I said, not to anyone in particular.

"It's fine," snapped Freddie.

"No, something's very wrong. People wouldn't just leave their cars like this without a reason."

Everyone stopped to look at me. Freddie didn't hide the contempt on his face.

I continued, "Don't you smell that?"

"What is it?" Jamie asked scrunching up her nose.

"Decaying flesh," Daniel answered. His gaze met mine and I saw the realization of how much danger we were in dawn on his face.

"It's really potent, there's got to be a lot of them around."

"Well, where are the bastards then?" Freddie asked condescendingly.

As if waiting for an introduction, the moaning became audible. It wasn't that close but it wasn't that far either. I turned to see the zombies coming out of the jungle that lined the road we were on. They were maybe 30 feet away from us.

"Shit," Daniel said.

I'd never seen them in a group before. Their slow movement didn't seem so slow when they were all together. Like they were pushing each other forward or were in a race to get to food first. Whatever it was, it made my heart feel like it had stopped in my chest. I felt like I was dead right there.

"Come on," Phoebe said as she grabbed my hand, pulling me back into reality.

I followed behind them as we made our way quickly through the cars.

"Over there," Daniel said pointing to the mall. It was only a few yards away from us. Close enough to feel like a blessing, yet far enough away to seem like a curse.

We made our way between the cars to the small hill that led down to the mall parking lot.

I couldn't help myself but when we reached the bottom of the hill, I looked back to see where the zombies were. I know I would've been a pillar of salt for sure. The zombies were having a hard time navigating the cars. It gave us time but only a few more precious seconds.

I continued running. The group was a few paces ahead of me but not far.

The zombies behind us were not our only friends. There were zombies coming at us from the right as well. They must have been in the parking lot across the street from the mall. They didn't have speed to speak of either but they didn't have as many cars to cut through as the ones behind us did.

Jamie noticed the group to the right and tripped in front of me. I helped her up. She was bleeding from her arm where she scraped it. The small amount of blood was all it took. The moaning intensified and I could've sworn those zombies picked up the pace as much as their decaying bodies would allow.

"Thanks," Jamie said.

"You're welcome," I said pulling her along as I ran to catch up with the rest of the group.

They had already reached the entrance of the mall. Daniel was trying to open the door but had no luck. They were locked.

"Damn it," he said.

"Just break the glass," Freddie said.

"No," said Robert. "We don't have time to find anything to block the door with. Or time to block the door for that matter."

"We've got to be able to get in," Phoebe said, sounding a bit panicked.

The zombies were getting closer. We didn't have much time.

I noticed an emergency exit to the side only about ten feet from where we stood.

"Let's go there," I said.

I led the way to the emergency exit. We caught a huge break. The door had been propped open with a rock. We all hurried inside letting the door shut behind us.

Daniel lit a flashlight, illuminating the long hallway we stood within. We all took a second to catch our breath. I leaned against the wall. Phoebe crouched down with her head on her knees as Robert rubbed her back. Daniel drank water and I noticed Freddie looked a bit unnerved.

I handed Jamie a band aid from my first aid kit. It was the mom in me coming out.

"Thanks," Jamie said with a smile and put the band aid on over her scrape. "Someone propped that door open," She said. "They might be coming back."

"It's too risky James," Robert said, still rubbing Phoebe's back. "There are dozens of those creatures out there. We can't risk them getting in here and if someone's out there, they're not getting through that crowd."

Jamie looked upset but said nothing. She just crossed her arms and leaned against the wall. Daniel put an arm around her and whispered something into her ear. She turned towards him and hugged him.

The banging on the door began from the outside. The zombies had caught up to us.

"Do you think they can get in?" Phoebe asked, looking up but still hugging her knees.

"No, I doubt they can." Daniel said. "Shall we?"

He began to move forward and the rest of us began to follow him down the long dark hallway into the unknown.

Chapter 12

We made it about halfway down the hallway when we came across what must have been some kind of storage area. The big double doors were chained shut from our side. There was dark, almost black blood on the chains and across the door. A big bang came from inside. Then the moaning started. They could sense food on the other side. I swallowed hard. I heard Jamie let out a yelp. Phoebe shushed her.

I noticed someone had written "Don't Open" in black marker across the doors. It was written so big that there was no way anyone could miss the message.

"Let's hope that's the only ones in here," Daniel said.

We continued through the dark hallway leaving the banging and moaning behind us. I felt the goose bumps all over my body. I had an uneasy chill running down my spine.

We made it to the end of the hall and went carefully through the door letting us out into the mall. All the stores were still open but there was no one left in the building except the undead it seemed.

It was decided that we would try the sporting goods store for safety. I think it was also for the potential stuff we could find to help in our journey. I wasn't happy that we would be settling in for the night but it's not like we had any other options with the hoard of zombies outside.

"There's no way they got all the zombies," Freddie said.

I hated to say that I thought he might be right.

"Just be observant and cautious. I do agree that this seems a little too perfect," Daniel replied

"It might be alright," Phoebe suggested. "I don't hear anything."

There were no noises coming from anywhere, which in a mall was a little weird. I'd never been in an empty mall and it was extremely unsettling.

We made our way upstairs and past the food court. Robert suggested after settling in we should have a team raid the food court for dinner so we wouldn't have to get into our food supply. Leave it to the chef to have the best plan involving the food supply.

It didn't take long to get to the sporting goods store. There were already two tents set up for display, so it wasn't necessary for us to use ours.

Robert, Daniel, and Phoebe decided to be the raiding food team. I was disappointed to be left with Freddie and his negative attitude. Jamie seemed to be overwhelmed by everything that was going on so I knew she wasn't going to talk much. I wasn't worried about help with the watch since the plan was to keep the gate closed while they were gone.

After they left, Jamie retreated into one of the tents. Freddie joined her.

I walked around the store, listening carefully for any sign of the undead. I didn't want to sit still for I was scared I would fall asleep. My emotions had made me exhausted. If I kept busy I could ignore it for the most part. I knew then I probably should have gone with the group raiding the food court because there was only so much to look at in the store.

I noticed some blood by a display of hiking boots. The uneasy feeling that was just staying at bay now came up to the surface. I pulled out the gun from my holster and followed the trail of blood. It led to a storage room in the back. There was blood all over the floor in front of the door and on the handle.

I reached out and opened it with caution. There was a zombie sitting on the floor with what looked like guts all over its lap. It was still eating from the pile of intestines and didn't seem to notice me open the door.

I decided shooting it might be a mistake. The noise would be too loud and might draw other zombies that might be hidden away. I put the gun the holster and took out my knife. I went up to the zombie. It looked up then and growled at me. It made to move for me but I stabbed it through the skull before it could. It stopped moving immediately. I pulled out the knife and cleaned it with a towel on one of the shelves.

"Is everything alright?"

I jumped at the sound of the male voice. I turned around trying to catch my breath. My heart was racing. Which I realized was ridiculous; a zombie wouldn't ask if everything was alright.

Though a zombie might've been a more welcoming sight than that of Freddie who stood in the doorway.

"Sorry," he said.

"It's okay," I replied.

He nodded and looked at the zombie on the ground.

"Is that the only one?"

"I think so. I don't know where anymore would be. There's not a dressing room or anything."

"Yeah, that's true."

I came out of the storage room and walked awkwardly next to Freddie.

"How's Jamie?" I asked just trying to make small talk.

"Scared and I don't blame her. We shouldn't be out here. This was a stupid idea that Daniel had."

"Well, I'm happy you are. I'd be dead without you guys." I said and it was the truth.

He smirked, "Yeah, sure. You sure it's not because you're dying to bang Daniel?"

"Excuse me?" I asked taking aback by his suggestion.

"I saw you two talking earlier so don't try to deny it."

"What exactly is your problem? Do you go out of your way to be this much of an asshole or is it just a natural part of your ugly personality?"

Freddie began laughing.

"This is funny?"

"Yeah, because I had no idea just how bad you wanted him."

"Look, my husband was just killed by a zombie. So no, I'm not looking to hook up with Daniel. Just because a woman and a man were talking doesn't mean that one of them wants to have sex with the other. Case in point, this conversation right here because all I want to do is punch you in your face."

His face changed from his smug look to one of concern, "I had no idea. I'm sorry."

"Instead of saying you're sorry, which is crap, how about you just stop running your damn mouth about shit you know nothing about."

He nodded but said nothing.

"Everything alright?" Jamie asked making her way towards us.

Freddie looked at me as he said, "Yeah, Shelly just ran into a zombie that's all. Just one, she killed it. We'll be fine."

Jamie looked worried but said nothing. She just turned and headed back for the tent. Freddie followed Jamie's path.

I leaned up against the wall and rested my head against it. I didn't know which was worse the undead or the living.

Chapter 13

I made my way over to the camp fire display and sat down. I had an attraction to Daniel that was true but the last thing on my mind was sleeping with him. The suggestion of such made me angry and annoyed. As if sex would be on the forefront of anyone's mind in a time like this.

I heard voices coming from down the hall. It sounded like them but I waited until they were in sight before opening the gate.

"How'd it go?" I asked. "Find anything good?"

"There wasn't a lot to choose from. Place has been picked almost clean." Phoebe said.

"I'd hate to see the super markets." I said.

"I got enough to make y'all a good meal, don't you worry," Robert added.

"Anything happen here?" Daniel asked.

"Zombie in a closet, eating some guts. Other than that it was pretty uneventful." I said closing the gate back down.

"There was a zombie in here?" Phoebe asked.

"Yeah, but we should be alright. Just need to stay vigilant." I replied.

Phoebe nodded but looked concerned. She busied herself helping Robert.

"Those two come out at all?" Daniel asked indicating the tent Freddie and Jamie were in.

"Just to see what was going on with the zombie." I lied and added. "I think Jamie is having a hard time with all of this."

"Yeah, I know." Daniel said and headed towards the back of the store.

Robert kept his word about the food. He made us a make shift shepherd's pie out of hot dog and hamburger buns, veggies they had found at a sandwich shop and some canned meat. It was surprisingly good though not as good as breakfast had been.

We decided on the watches. I volunteered to go first with Robert since I knew once I laid down it would be hard for me to get back up so I thought it best to get the watch out of the way. Not that it was nearly as dangerous as outside would be, especially with the gates closed but we all figured it would be best to still do a watch. Daniel and Phoebe insisted on it especially after hearing about the zombie in the closet.

Before going to bed we took turns going to the rest room which was only a few feet from the store.

Phoebe, Jamie, and I went first. There were ten stalls and most of them were completely disgusting. I wasn't surprised by it and Phoebe didn't really seem fazed but Jamie was more than a little sick to the stomach over the sight of it. There was one very clean stall, almost immaculate at the end. We took turns using that one. The water was still on which I didn't expect.

Jamie went first while Phoebe and I brushed our teeth.

"Robert keeps mentioning something about a typhoon," Phoebe said with toothpaste in her mouth.

"What?" I asked.

"Yeah, he wants to get to the caves ASAP because of a typhoon they said was building off the coast."

"When? When, when did they say that? I don't remember anything about a typhoon."

"Neither do I but with all the undead running around, there's a strong chance it was over looked or forgotten."

"So you're telling me that there is a typhoon headed for us?"

"Possibly, but Robert might be remembering wrong or just extremely paranoid."

I let out a sigh, "does he remember when they said it might hit?"

"At the end of the week possibly."

I scratched my forehead, "so, like in two days?"

"That's what he keeps saying."

Jamie flushed the toilet. Phoebe and I stopped talking, as if she couldn't hear us.

"I feel terrible," she said walking to the sink and turning on the water.

Phoebe didn't say anything, she just headed to the toilet, saying "I'm next," as she headed for the stall.

I looked at Jamie's face in the mirror, something wasn't right.

"Are you okay?" I asked.

"Just my stomach," she said as she dried her hands. "And my head, and my muscles, and every other part of me."

Tears began to run down her face. I walked over and gave her a hug. She wrapped her arms around me in a tight embrace.

"I'm so scared," she gasped. "I feel like I'm going to fall apart because of it. The terror is so strong."

"It's going to be okay. We're going to be okay," I said but didn't really believe it.

"You're not scared?" she asked pulling away from me and looking at my eyes.

"Yes, I am completely terrified. But giving in to fear gets you nowhere right?"

She gave a weak smile, "yeah, that's right."

Phoebe came out of the stall.

"Sorry, I had to pee."

"It's alright," I said.

We finished up what we needed to do and headed back to the store. The guys let us in the gate and headed out themselves. Robert gave Phoebe a kiss before going. Freddie didn't even look at Jamie.

After they left, Phoebe climbed into one of the tents.

"Night, girls. I'm beat."

"Goodnight," I said.

Jamie smiled and said "Night, night."

I sat on the log in the makeshift camp sight.

"I heard what Freddie said to you earlier," Jamie said. She continued when I looked at her confused. "About my brother."

"Oh, that."

"I'm sorry. He can be bit crude," she said.

"You sure do apologize for him a lot."

She shrugged, "he's just not good with people."

"You mean he's not a good person."

"He is, deep down. You wouldn't understand," she said looking down at her feet.

I sighed, "I understand. It's hard when you love someone to always see them clearly. Believe me I know."

She nodded, "well, it wasn't nice what he said to you. He's jealous of Daniel. I don't really know why."

"Well, now's the time for him to man up and stop being such a baby."

She laughed, "Yeah. That's not going to happen though. Goodnight."

"Night," I said.

She went into the other tent and zipped it shut.

The guys came back shortly after Jamie had gone into the tent. We closed and locked up the gate. Freddie settled in with her without saying much to anyone. Daniel, Robert, and I sat around chatting a little before Daniel went to sleep. He had set up his sleeping bag off to the side of the two tents instead of sleeping in one. I think he wanted to be ready at a moment's notice if he needed to be.

      Robert and I set together with the lantern on. We didn't talk much. Robert seemed to be deep in thought and I was just trying to stay awake for the three hours our watch lasted. Volunteering to go first I realized might have been a mistake.

      "Strange how life has turned out, isn't it?" Robert said.

      I nodded, "strange indeed."

      Robert was about to reply when there was a sudden burst of laughter. It was coming from down the hall.

Chapter 14

Robert looked at me. He pointed behind the counter where the cash register was. I made my way over to the counter and crouched behind it. Robert picked up the lantern and followed me. When he got in position in front of me, he turned the lantern off.

We sat in silence waiting for whatever it was. I could only hear Robert's breathing and the deep breaths of the others sleeping in the tents. Then the laughter echoed off the hall. It sounded unnatural and unreal given the situation the world was in. It was something you would expect to hear in a mall on a Saturday afternoon from a bunch of teenagers.

I wondered if these people had been here awhile and if they had known we were here. What if this was part of a sick game and now that the world had about come to an end, they were going to go on a killing spree of the few people that were still kicking?

"Let's go sleep in the hammock store," a girl said. Her voice was echoing in the open space. "I've always wanted to do that."

"Could you take this a bit more seriously? We were almost attacked by those things." Said another girl.

"Yeah, but we weren't so let's enjoy what we can."

I saw the light from their flash light. They came into view in front of the store. I almost thought it was only the two of them until a boy joined them in front of the store.

"Come on Laci, we're safe for tonight." He said.
He looked at the store we were in. Robert and I moved more behind the counter just in case they shined the light in. I was worried someone was going to wake up and give us away.

Daniel couldn't be seen from that angle where he was sleeping thankfully.

"Why is the gate down on this store but none of the others?" the boy asked.

I felt my blood run cold when he said that. I just knew we were done for.

"It's probably to cage in those ugly things." One of the girls replied.

"No, they would be trying to get us. There are people in there." He said his voice sounded sinister. "Come out, come out and play whoever you are." He then began to laugh.

There was a smacking sound.

"What the hell did you do that for?" He shouted.

"You're going to get us killed. If someone is in there that's alive, which I highly doubt, they'll probably kill us. It's not like we have anything to defend ourselves with."

"Look, I was just being funny, you're so damn uptight. Let's go."

Their footsteps started and faded into the distance.

I heard a zipper.

"What was that?" Phoebe whispered.

"Just some stupid teenagers," Robert replied. "They won't hurt us."

Phoebe nodded and went back in the tent after Robert's reassurances. Robert and I went back to where we were guarding near the front of the store. He only turned on the lantern to guide our way back then shut it off to keep from being noticed.

"How do you think they got past all those zombies outside?" I asked, curious beyond belief considering that they had said they had no weapons.

"They've probably moved on from there. It's been awhile. Regardless the reason, it sounds promising for us tomorrow."

We kept guard for two more hours. There were no more occurrences. The teenagers settled in somewhere because they never came back and there were no appearances from any zombies either.

After we were done with our watch, we woke up Phoebe and Daniel. Robert gave them the watch to keep track of time and we switched places. I took the tent and Robert the other sleeping bag.

I was completely exhausted even my bones were tired. I was out almost as soon as I laid my body down. However, my sleep was not the most restful. I never woke up but I had strange dreams involving being attacked at a drive thru by Jackie. Then it lead into seeing Adam and Julie together before they both became Zombies and tried to attack me, then it formed into a dream involving Daniel that had absolutely nothing to do with zombies.

I woke up feeling scared and uneasy. I took a long drink of water for my mouth was completely dry.

I unzipped and exited the tent. Everyone else was awake and eating sandwiches for breakfast, since they wouldn't keep very long.

"Good morning," Phoebe and Jamie said at the same time then erupted in a fit of giggles.

"Morning," I said sitting down and fixing myself a sandwich.

"How'd you sleep?" Robert asked.

"I slept alright. Did those kids ever appear again?" I asked.

"Not during our watch," Phoebe replied.

"We heard some noise coming from down the hall but we never saw anyone," Freddie said. "They might have headed out the other way though."

I was surprised he spoke of his and Jamie's watch instead of Jamie. He almost sounded like a human.

"Not to rush you but we need to get going and make up time." Daniel stated.

Phoebe said, "We'll be alright. We can walk fast."

"It's alright, we can get ready." I agreed. I ate my sandwich as we got everything together. I wanted to get to the Navy Base.

It didn't take long to get our stuff together since we didn't need to set up our own tents.

Phoebe unlocked the gate and lifted it. We headed out cautiously but it appeared that no one else was in the building anymore.

Though we decided to go back the way we came. The food court was trashed. There was food and condiments everywhere. I doubted Daniel, Robert, and Phoebe had left it like that.

Phoebe shook her head, "That's what I probably would've done if I was a teenager in the zombie apocalypse."

"I'm surprised you didn't do it now," Daniel teased.

Phoebe smacked his stomach before descending down the stairs.

We made it to the locked front doors. We wanted to see what we were heading out into before we took the emergency exit. There were no signs of any zombies but the sky looked angry. It looked very odd for Guam. I knew then that what Phoebe had said about the typhoon was probably true. If we got caught in a huge storm, would we be able to find shelter in time?

Since no one else made any fuss about it I decided not to worry. There was enough to worry about without worrying about a storm that probably wouldn't hit anyway.

We walked out of the exit. The air was heavy and extremely humid. I felt the sweat form around my hairline and almost all over my body immediately. I drank a lot of water. Probably more than I should have since I was supposed to be conserving my water.

We were all quiet as we made our way. I could tell I wasn't the only one affected by the humidity but no one was complaining.

"Does the weather seem odd to anyone else?" I asked.

"Are you overheated?" Freddie asked.

"No, something is off."

"I'm telling you that typhoon they reported is going to hit us," said Robert.

Daniel stopped, "I don't think so. We're probably getting an effect from it but I don't think it will hit us full on."

"I think you're being unrealistic." Robert said, "those things have a mind of their own it could easily change course again."

"Let's just focus on not getting eaten by zombies and cross the typhoon bridge if and when we come to it." Daniel said.

Nobody said anything else about a possible typhoon and we continued on. We weren't making great time though. We were trying to stay on the main road but the deserted cars seemed to span the rest of the Island. Who knows what people were thinking, there were only so many places to go. Perhaps it was just a state of panic or fear. After all, fear was what seemed to be keeping me running.

Then it happened. It seemed to go so damn fast. A zombie appeared out of the jungle to our right. Daniel caught sight of it and managed to stab it in the head without any problem but the zombie wasn't alone. I was learning fast that they often traveled in packs.

The next zombie, Phoebe took out. I got my own to deal with. In no time we were outnumbered by this mass wave of zombies intent on eating our insides. Yet we managed to hold strong it seemed. Everyone was stabbing and dodging their way through. We were going to make it, I could feel it. We were going to be alright.

That's when Jamie's voice filled the air. A loud high pitched piercing sound that sent chills through the bone. I couldn't stop what I was doing to look because a zombie had grabbed on to my shirt and was biting at me but I knew it couldn't be good.

I finally managed to get the upper hand in my dark dance with the undead and got my hunting knife through the temple of the zombie.

I looked over just as Daniel yelled "Jamie," and rushed over to her.

She was covered in her own blood from a neck wound and fell to the ground. Phoebe stabbed the zombie that got her in back of the skull.

Freddie seemed to be frozen in shock. She was done. She would be one of them in only a little bit of time.

Daniel was kneeling next to her.

"Jamie," he said. "You're going to be alright."

She choked out, " I love you guys." She was having hard time breathing and closed her eyes.

"No, no, no! Jamie, please no." Daniel cried.

We were all almost done at that second as this tragedy taking place seemed to paralyze us. Phoebe was crying, Freddie hadn't moved and the sight of another death in such a short span of time almost knocked me down. I didn't know Jamie that well but she was a nice person and so young. I would wonder after if she hadn't done herself in with her belief that she didn't stand a chance.

The only thing that saved us was Robert hadn't lost his focus. He had killed several zombies on his own before he yelled out.

"We've got to keep fighting."

I turned around just in time to stop the zombie behind me, with another one only a few steps behind it.

Daniel hadn't moved from Jamie's dead body. He was crying next to her. Freddie was no longer frozen. He was fighting along with Phoebe, Robert, and me. When I was able to look though, I did see that he was crying.

We were not out of our bad fortune. Daniel composed himself and joined our fight. The five of us were fighting so hard that none of us saw it coming.

Robert didn't scream, he didn't make a noise at all. It wasn't until I heard a zombie growls more animated behind me that I even noticed. I turned and saw a zombie chewing on Robert's right shoulder.

"Damn it," I said.

I ran over and stabbed the zombie in the head. Robert fell to the ground, his eyes glazed over. The zombie had gotten his throat first and pulled out a huge chunk of it.

The others finished off the remaining group of the undead killers before they noticed.

"Oh my God," Phoebe said. "Not Robert. Not him, please."

Daniel went over and hugged Phoebe.

I watched Freddie walk over and kneel next to Jamie's body. He stroked Jamie's arm.

"This is all your fault," he spat out.

Daniel let go of Phoebe. She wiped her eyes. I walked over and put my arm around her because she didn't look like she could stand without support.

"What?" Daniel asked.

"You heard me," Freddie said. "You know I'm right. This is your fault."

"I just lost my sister and best friend. I'd watch it if I were you."

"This was your stupid idea. If it wasn't for you, they might still be alive."

"It wasn't safe there. Everyone but you understood that," Daniel yelled.

"It was safer than this and now Jamie and Robert are dead because of your stupidity."

Daniel punched Freddie in the mouth. Freddie tried to hit back but Daniel ducked. Daniel then took Freddie down and they were fighting on the ground.

"Stop it," I said letting go of Phoebe. "You're going to attract more of those undead things and then we'll all be dead."

The scuffle continued for another minute before they broke apart.

Freddie was bleeding heavily from his nose and mouth. Daniel, being the clear winner, only had a busted lip.

"I'm not continuing on this pointless journey," Freddie barked.

"Then go," Daniel said back.

"He'll never make it by himself," I stated.

"If he wants to go, I'm not going to stop him."

Freddie shook his head and backed away from us. He grabbed his bag off the ground. He then turned and headed of in the other direction.

I was shocked at the turn of events and knowing he wouldn't make it made me want to vomit. I understood the raw emotions that Daniel was feeling to let him just leave especially being told his sister's death was his fault but I just couldn't believe it. We had started out as six barely 3 hours prior and now our group was cut in half. We weren't much better off than Freddie.

"We need to go," Daniel said.

It was true that we couldn't stay there but we couldn't get Phoebe to leave. She was sitting down next to Roberts's body. She picked some wild flowers next to her and placed them around his body. She began humming to herself.

Daniel didn't say anything though I could see the panic on his face. He was keeping his eyes peeled around the surrounding area. We couldn't just stay and wait for an attack.

Then the weather gave us the push. It started to rain, hard and fast. It wasn't like the everyday rain we were used to. We all knew too well what it was the start of. Robert and I had been right to be concerned but it felt like another damn blow to an already fragile system.

"Come on, Phoebe, we've got to find shelter." Daniel said.

"No, I can't leave him," she replied. "I can't. I won't."

"Phoebe," Daniel pleaded.

"Go," she said. "Leave me here."

Determined not to lose a fourth person today, I went over to her, "Phoebe, I know how you feel, everything inside of you feels ripped out and dead but it's not. We have to go, there's a typhoon approaching. We need you if we have any hope to survive, please. You have more to live for than I do, I know you're strong enough to make it."

She let out a small whimper and nodded. "Okay."

She kissed the side of Robert's cheek and got up.

We began running with no real direction, just trying to find somewhere, anywhere that we might be safe.

It wasn't going to be easy; the area we were in was mostly jungle. The rain was pouring down on us and was making visibility almost nonexistent. I could really only make out the green foliage to the side of me and Phoebe running just a foot ahead of me.

It was bad and I was running out of breath after the fight we had just encountered and now running. I wanted to throw in the towel, just lie down and let the rain wash over my body.

"Over there," Daniel yelled.

I assumed he was pointing to somewhere but I couldn't make him out in the rain. He was too far ahead of me. I just kept Phoebe in sight and when she made a sharp turn to the left, I followed.

My foot hit a hole in the ground but I managed to keep my balance by some miracle. I also didn't twist my ankle which was an amazing feat.

We passed through a stable. It was empty. I didn't know what happened to the horses and I didn't want to know. Given the state of things, they had probably been turned into zombie food which was just another depressing thought.

I really didn't know how I was going to make it in this new world where every scenario just made me sad. Would I or any of us ever experience happiness again? Would we remember how to laugh as things got worse? It was heartbreaking and gutwrenching to think about but it was the truth.

We passed through the stable to a tiny walkway between one of the stables and a shed that must have held some yard equipment. There was a tiny house that lay ahead.

We were all on the porch when Daniel knocked. There was no answer. He knocked again. Still no one came to the door.

Daniel turned the knob and it was unlocked. We all had weapons up just in case there were any undead creatures inside waiting to devour us.

"Hello," Daniel called out. "Is anyone here?"

There was no response. The windows had been bordered up to protect from either the storm or the zombies, so it didn't make any sense why someone would leave.

"I'll check around," Daniel said.

It wouldn't take long; it was more a shack than a house. There was a tiny kitchen off the main room we had walked into. There was probably only one bedroom and bathroom. The main room we came into had a dirty blue couch sat against a wall with an even dirtier green chair to the side of it. There was an old TV against the opposite wall and a tiny bookcase.

Daniel came back after a few minutes.

"All clear," he said. "Let's get this place locked up."

We shut the door and locked it. Daniel tied it off with some rope that was in their camping gear. We all helped move the bookcase in front of the door to keep it from being opened.

"Is there a back door?" I asked.

"No, this is the only way in. All the windows are boarded up as well. I don't know why they left, they made this place safe."

"You think they might come back?" I asked.

Daniel shook his head, "No, the closet is a mess as well as the dresser. They packed and left in a hurry it looks like."

"Why?"

"I'd like to know that myself. There are no zombies in here and it doesn't look like there ever was."

"They probably attacked the animals and the owner freaked," Phoebe said as she plopped down into the yucky green chair.

There wasn't much light so Daniel lit up one of the lanterns and sat it on the table.

Phoebe looked completely different, the cost of her loss visible on her face. Daniel had sat down at the table, his face in deep sorrow. It was a room full of grief. I couldn't take it.

I took my things into the bathroom and shut the door. I put my bag down on the floor and sat on the toilet. I was soaked to the bone and I had come in here to change but I needed a moment to myself. I didn't know these people well but they were kind enough to take me along with their group and now two of them were dead and another gone to meet the same fate. The death was taking its toll on me. I'd lost my family and watched as three others lost their loved ones. Who was next because there was no way we were going to make it. It was like a game of Russian Rolette except you would never stop playing until the bullet got you. There was no way to beat the zombies, not really. If a cure could be found it was going to be next to impossible, since I'm sure most research places were all but inoperable. We were living in the plague of the dead and the dead were winning.

I got some clothes out of my bag and changed. The clothes I shed I put on the shower rail to dry. I walked out of the bathroom to find Daniel in the same spot only there was a bottle of whiskey open in front of him. Phoebe was not in the room.

"Where's phoebe?" I asked.

"She went into the bedroom to be alone," he said. "Drink?"

I nodded, "yeah."

Chapter 15

I sat down at the table as Daniel poured me a drink. He put the glass down in front of me. It was a filthy glass. There was dust on it, like it hadn't been used in ages. I didn't let that stop me. I also didn't let the fact that I hated Whiskey stop me either. I downed the whole glass in one long gulp. It burned my insides on the ride down to my stomach. The taste was disgusting but I needed that burn.

Daniel had a quizzical look on his face. "More?"

I put the glass in front of him, "Yes, please."

He poured more of the whiskey into the filthy glass. I drank this one a bit slower than the last. Daniel was still working on his first glass. We sat in silence as we nursed our liquid medicine. I felt like we were in our own separate glass boxes of grief. I felt worlds away yet very much present. Maybe it was the alcohol. I hadn't had a real drink in ages so my tolerance was nonexistent.

The storm was raging outside by this time. The house creaked as the wind outside picked up. It was loud and obnoxious sounding. My fear would've been at a dangerously high level if it wasn't for the numbing effect of the whiskey. I was extremely relaxed.

"This is a mess," Daniel stated.

"Tell me about it," I said in agreement.

"You think we'll make it? What are we fighting for at this point?" he asked.

I laughed at the complexity of his questions in my tipsy state. "I don't know. I think we're lucky to have made it this far."

"Yeah, and luck eventually runs out."

"Man, you are a downer when you drink," I said.

He laughed a little. "I guess I am."

I finished off my second glass. I felt immediately drowsy. I yawned for a long moment.

"I'm exhausted," I stated.

"Go, get some sleep," he stated. "We're as safe as we can possibly be."

I nodded, "Yeah, which isn't that safe."

He smiled, "No, it's not."

"But I'm completely relaxed right now. So thank you for sharing that wonderful drink that I hate; but I kind of love it at the moment. I am going to lie down on that couch over there."

"Okay, enjoy." He said with a grin.

"Oh, you have no idea," I said as I stood up. I swayed a bit as I got up.

Daniel made to get up to help me but I waved him away.

"I'm fine, just not all together now."

"You're a little drunk," he said and laughed.

"I need to be drunk right now. This has been hell."

He nodded, "it has indeed."

"You think we're being punished?" I asked. I lost my balance and caught myself on the chair.

Daniel eyed me for a moment to make sure I was alright before answering.

"I don't think you deserve to be punished."

"I didn't ask if I deserved it, I asked if we were being punished."

He thought a moment, "maybe as human beings but I don't think we personally are being punished."

I nodded not really following what he was saying because my head was beginning to swim.

"Alright, I'm going to go lay down. You should probably sleep too."

"Someone's got to keep watch."

"I think we're fine but do what you need to do."

I walked away from the table slowly. I was walking wobbly as I made my way to the couch. I grabbed my bag from where I dropped in next to the chair.

I pulled out Jackie's blanket and set the bag back down on the floor. I laid my body down on the dirty couch. My eyes closed instantly, maybe before my head hit the dirty pillow. My body was thankful to not be moving anymore. I felt like I was floating on air. I was so past exhausted at this point and the alcohol had relaxed my mind enough to finally let me rest. I didn't think about how I just wanted to stop running, stop hiding, and stop fighting. I didn't think about if I was ever going to make it to the Navy base. I went to sleep quickly to the lullaby of the storm.

I didn't dream at all. It was the first time I slept since this mess started that my subconscious didn't send me a counter attack in my dreams.

I wasn't asleep very long before I woke up. I needed to use the restroom bad and that pulled me out of my beautiful restful state. It was late though, I could tell that much in the pitch black of the room. The lantern was turned off. After my eyes adjusted to the dark, I could make out Daniel's body in the middle of the floor. I could also hear his heavy breathing.

I was happy that he decided to get some rest as well. Perhaps the whiskey had done the deciding for him but whatever it was, it was a good thing. I knew we should probably have one person awake but we needed our rest after the events of the day. We were never going to be safer than we were in this shack so we might as well take advantage.

I made my way to the bathroom. The storm outside had not lost any of its strength. It was just as loud if not louder as before. I thought that perhaps zombies were caught up in the wind, being blown around the island. With any luck, maybe their undead bodies would be tossed into the Pacific by the storm that was raging on still. It was a silly thought but it made me smile none the less.

I finished up in the bathroom and made my way slowly back to the couch to get more sleep. I had a slight headache but I was too exhausted to care.

As I made my way back, I could hear the faint sound of crying. It was Phoebe in the bedroom. My heart broke for her. I thought about going in to talk to her but then decided not to. I'd go in in the morning. Right now, she probably didn't want to see anyone.

As I got back to the couch, I grabbed my gun out of my bag. I set it on the table next to me just to be safe. In case somehow a zombie made to the inside of the house.

I laid back down and went back to sleep. I was not so lucky this time. My subconscious was no longer numbed by the alcohol.

I dreamed of Jackie. I dreamed about her birthday party and at the party, amongst the girls dressed in their Disney Princess finest she became a zombie. She attacked her friends, then their parents. I watched in horror as she devoured Adam in front of me. Then she turned her dead grey eyes towards me. I was pleading "Jackie, its mommy. Please Jackie." But it made no difference. She opened her mouth to reveal her yellow teeth and lunged. I screamed.

The scream was only inside my head because Daniel was not awakened by it. I breathed deeply and gained my senses back. It was only a terrible dream but it shook me to my very core. It cut me down through my gut. I figured I wouldn't be going back to sleep for a while.

I was right. I didn't fall asleep for a long time. I didn't dwell on the dream but I did think about Cate. At this point it was a safe bet that all hope was gone of getting off the island. It was too late. I suddenly felt like I was in prison. I guess there are worse things than being imprisoned on a beautiful island but I hated the feeling of being trapped. My world had collapsed around my feet and there was nothing I could do to change it. With that realization, I longed for the nightmare I had awoken from.

I did eventually fall back asleep. Though it was not restful, I didn't have any dreams that I remembered which I was thankful for.

I probably would've slept for days had I not been woken up by the sound of glass shattering.

Chapter 16

"Damn it! You're got to be kidding me with this shit," Daniel said getting to his feet.

"What is it?" I asked sitting up.

"Not entirely sure but it can't be good. Can you help me with this?" He asked indicating the bookcase.

"Yeah," I said getting up from the couch.

"What's going on?" Phoebe asked appearing in the bedroom doorway.

"That's what we're trying to figure out," Daniel answered.

Phoebe said nothing else; she came over to help us move the bookcase. She didn't make eye contact with either of us. I could tell though that her eyes were blood shot. I felt bad for her and wanted to give her a hug but we had to deal with the task at hand.

With a bit of effort we got the bookcase out of the way. While Daniel untied the door, I grabbed my knife out of my bag.

I followed Daniel out onto the little porch. Phoebe stood in the doorway.

I looked around. The sky looked angry. Trees had fallen and I noticed that the shed was missing some of its panels. The air was thick and heavy. The storm seemed to be over but the humidity was awful.

I hadn't seen Daniel grab his gun but he was also armed.

"What the hell?" Daniel said.

He bent down and picked up a giant brown and grey rock that was lying below the window in a pile of glass.

"How did that not knock out the boards on the inside?" Phoebe asked observing the size and the density of the rock.

"Someone threw that right?" I asked.

"Had to have, I just don't understand who," Daniel said.

"Think maybe the owners," I suggested.

"Isn't it obvious," Phoebe said. She was leaning against the door frame. "That was Freddie."

I looked at Daniel's face. He had a look that spoke volumes. He obviously didn't think that was possible.

"No way," he said. Speaking what I thought I saw written on his face.

"It's him," Phoebe stated. "I can feel it in my bones."

"That means he would've been following us and where was he when the storm hit?" I asked.

Phoebe looked a bit exasperated that we didn't agree with her theory.

"Well, a zombie didn't throw that rock at the window."

Daniel nodded. "Phoebe you stay inside. I'll check out the back, Shelly you get the front."

"Okay," Phoebe and I said in unison.

Phoebe shut the door while Daniel headed round back. I stepped out into the yard. It was hot and muggy. I felt like I was walking into an oven. I was sweating ridiculously and my clothes were sticking to me.

I walked out further into the yard. I got an eerie feeling in the pit of my stomach. I was concerned about the zombies popping out from behind the bushes or the shed. Where were they anyway?

I stepped on a stick that cracked loudly; I stood still to see if I attracted any zombies. After there were no undead creatures trying to get me, I continued on.

I heard a rustle of leaves from the plants in front of me. I brought my knife up, ready to attack.

"Hello?" I said cautiously.

I heard a laugh come from the plants.

Freddie came out from behind the plants. Phoebe had been right. I brought the knife down to my side.

"Freddie? What are you doing here?"

"Just thought I'd confront some people who needed confronting," he said. He had a strange look on his face.

"What are you talking about?" I asked.

"Daniel needs to pay for what he's done."

"He hasn't done anything," I stated.

He scoffed at me, "Of course you would defend him. He got the love of my life killed."

"That was his sister dumbass. And you sure didn't act like you loved her that much."

He looked angry then. He stepped forward. I took a step away from him. He noticed this and grinned maliciously.

"What are you scared of Shelly?"

I felt my blood go cold and I knew then I needed to get away from him. I turned the opposite direction and began to run.

I wasn't fast enough. He caught up to me and knocked me to the ground. My knife went flying out of my hand. I flipped over and kicked him in the stomach. He grabbed his midsection in pain. I tried to get away but he latched his other hand around my ankle and dragged me back. He pinned my arms to the ground with his knees. I'd never been in so much pain.

"Stop it," he said. "You're going to enjoy this, trust me."

That's when I let out the loudest scream I could muster. Freddie slapped me hard.

"Shut up bitch. You want to attract every zombie around."

"That's exactly what I want," I said. "You can't rape me if your skin is being ripped off your bones by the living dead." I said and let out another scream.

He raised his hand to hit me again. Before he brought it back down, a grey face came and latched its teeth to his hand. The blood splattered down onto me.

Freddie yelled in pain. His attention was now on the zombie attacking him and he took his weight off of me.

I crawled to my knife and got up. I turned to see Freddie winning his fight with the zombie.

He turned towards me. "I can cut off my hand and be fine," he said.

I raised my knife to stab him as he began to walk forward. He took two steps and then I heard a gun go off. Blood shot out of a small hole in the center of Freddie's forehead and he slumped to the ground.

I turned to see Daniel with his .45 pointing at where Freddie had just stood. "Better safe than sorry," he said.

Chapter 17

Daniel walked over and helped me up from the ground.

"Thanks," I said as I wiped the dirt off of my shorts.

Phoebe came rushing over to me. I didn't see her open the door to come out.

"You alright?" She asked.

"I think so yeah."

I heard the sound of faint growling. We all looked at each other. We all knew without saying it, we needed to head back to the house and fast. We made our way quickly to the front porch.

I looked back before going in. A small herd of those creatures was coming from just past the stables. They looked to be maybe 25 feet away.

We hurried in and shut the door behind us. Daniel tied the door of with the rope. Phoebe and I helped him with the bookcase.

"Do you think our safety is compromised?" Phoebe asked pointing to the boarded up window Freddie had thrown the rock at.

"Doesn't look like it," Daniel said observing the wood more closely. "Just don't have that extra layer between us and the undead."

"I like that extra layer," I said,

I could hear the growling getting louder. Between the alcohol, the zombies, and being attacked I felt like I was going to be sick.

"Daniel, can you hold down the fort for a little while?" Phoebe asked.

Daniel looked at her a moment and nodded, "Yeah. I really think we're fine."

"Okay. Shelly, why don't you go take a shower and then join me in the other room," she said.

I nodded and Phoebe handed me my bag. I headed to the bathroom and took a cold shower. I felt disgusting with Freddie's blood on my face, although that was the least of why I felt disgusting.

I dried off and got dressed. I headed into the bedroom. She shut the door behind us and gave me a big hug.

"You really are alright?" she asked in my ear.

"I don't know," I said.

She let go of me, "Me either."

We both sat down on the bed. We were silent for a few minutes.

"He was really going to rape you?" she asked. "Wasn't he? I mean I always knew how much of a jerk he was but I never would've guessed he'd attempt something like that."

I shook my head, "I think something in him snapped. He looked strange. He was a bastard before but there was a sense of evil in him that was really creepy."

I didn't want to talk about it anymore. The mere thought of it made me feel ill. I was thankful it didn't go any further than it did. He didn't even rip my clothes. I was lucky. I wondered what other women surviving this crisis might be going through. Was it not only the undead that they had to fear?

"How are you holding up?" I asked Phoebe, desperate for the change of subject.

"I'm breathing. I guess that's as good as can be expected."

I nodded, "Yeah, it's not easy but you'll get up every day and catch your breath. Something inside you won't let you give up. Even at the worst of times, something deep inside will drive you to somehow stay alive."

She swallowed, "Did something happen to you? Did you lose someone?"

I nodded, "My daughter and my husband."

"I'm so sorry." She said as she sat up in the bed. "Why didn't you say anything?"

"I talked about it with Daniel but I really didn't want to bring too much attention to what I'd been through. Didn't want to seem weak you know? I didn't want to appear as broken as I felt."

"You could have said something. No one would think you were weak."

I smiled and gave her a hug.

Phoebe and I ended up talking for a long time. She told me stories about Robert. I let her do most of the talking. I did mention a few things here and there but I still wasn't ready to go into detail about my life with Jackie and Adam.

Both of us fell asleep after a little while. When I woke up, I was disoriented. I felt really bad to have left Daniel out there by himself for so long, protecting us from the zombies. Phoebe was still asleep so I quietly went to the bedroom door and walked into the main room.

Daniel was sitting on the floor on his sleeping bag when I came out of the room. He was facing the door covered by the bookcase.

"Hey," I began. "Everything alright?" I sat down next to him.

"Yeah, I could hear them eating on Freddie but most of the herd I think went on past the house. I heard like one or two on the porch but that was it."

I sighed with relief, "Good, I was worried. I didn't mean to fall asleep."

"It's alright. Both of you are pretty stressed out. How are you?"

"I'm fine."

"I'm sorry I didn't get there sooner," he said.

"He didn't do anything to me; just the intention has me unnerved."

He nodded. "That was smart to draw in a zombie like that."

"I was trying to get a zombie or you. I was worried I would draw in a horde of them which happened but I was at a loss of what to do."

"It worked. That's what matters." He said with a smile.

I sat down next to him and we began to talk for a while. He was trying to take my mind off what had happened I think. Phoebe was still asleep or at least she wasn't coming out of the room.

Daniel talked about his parents and his childhood. He told me a lot about Jamie. She was extremely smart and had been accepted into Yale but chose to move back to Guam and go to the University here. I didn't understand how someone so smart could end up with someone so terrible like Freddie. I didn't dwell on it though since the very thought of Freddie made me want to vomit.

Daniel and I talked about the shows we were going to miss like Family Guy and Elementary. We also talked about how we'd both miss watching baseball in the summer. It was bittersweet to reminisce. We had lost so much in such a short amount of time. Even the little stupid stuff was gone. We'd probably never enjoy a soda again. No fast food, movies, even surfing the web. It was all gone now.

It had gotten late and neither of us was ready to sleep. I knew we needed to since we planned to leave in the morning. Instead we just kept talking.

After a while I felt the air change, aware of the tension. I knew deep down it had been there all along but it still surprised me. I was of course attracted to him. However, I still felt like a married woman. As if I'd be doing something wrong to pay attention to the growing longing.

He leaned in first and I met him halfway. I was surprised by how tender his kiss was. It flowed so easy, his lips lining the curves of my neck. He knew all the right places to touch me.

Maybe it was being threatened by death so closely and I just wanted to feel alive and I gave in. I just needed to feel the heat of skin on skin. Feel the urgency and kiss of passion.

Afterwards Daniel fell asleep. I was too wired to sleep so I stayed awake and kept watch. I felt a bit strange about what had just happened between Daniel and me. I'd never been with anyone but Adam. It was weird but kind of nice too.

I sat in the dark listening to the wind outside. The rain had gone but the wind was still strong. I could hear the occasional moan of the dead. They didn't sound close to us. It sounded like the wind was picking up the voices. There was really no telling how close they might be.

Halfway through the night I heard something different, the shuffling of feet. I listened hard, trying to distinguish what I was hearing over the wind. It was close. The shuffling and the moans that followed. There was something dead on the porch.

I put my ear against the wall between the door and the window. I could hear nails scrapping along the other side of where I stood. It was right there, so close to us. I heard an angry groan and the scrapping and shuffling stopped.

I backed away from the wall. I had a feeling that dead creature on the other side sensed my presence. I got my gun ready just in case, though I felt strangely calm. I wasn't as scared as I should or had been in the previous encounters with these things. Maybe it became easier over time or maybe it was all the trauma I had been dealt since this mess started. Maybe dealing with the dead creatures wanting to eat my guts out was an easier thing to deal with than everything else that had come my way.

The dead creature must have lost its interest because I heard it shuffle the other way. Eventually the shuffling faded completely. I put my gun away. I would just tell Daniel and Phoebe what I heard when we left in the morning.

The morning, I hadn't thought about that. We were finally going to continue our journey in the morning and would split up somewhere along the way. I would finally make it to the Navy base.

The thing was, was there a point in continuing on to that destination? I didn't know anymore. It was the only thing that kept me going after the loss of my dear Jackie and Adam. It was what kept me breathing and surviving. It was the thing that kept me fighting.

So why give it up now? Was it worth it? Most likely they wouldn't let me on the Navy base or what might be left of it. They probably wouldn't have any ships leaving. So much time had passed now. Though, deep down I had to admit that staying now would have little to do with logic and all to do with emotion. I couldn't deny that if I stayed I'd be staying now because of having slept with Daniel. Was that anything more than a moment of pure human need? Would he be worth staying for? And what was love in a world like this anyway?

I knew I couldn't stay. I needed to try and get to Cate. That was my mission and I couldn't abandon it. I couldn't turn my back on what had kept me alive and kicking. I had to see it through, even if it was going to be failure.

Chapter 18

"Did you sleep?" Daniel asked as he packed a blue shirt back into his bag.

"No," I answered.

He looked at me for a long moment before he spoke. "Won't you be tired?"

"I'll be alright," I replied. "Besides it's not that far to the Navy base."

I looked at him and saw the look of surprise on his face, though his expression changed quickly.

"Yeah, that's true. Should be alright," he said as if the words were falling out of his mouth. "I'm going to check on Phoebe."

Daniel walked towards the bedroom and knocked on the door. I didn't hear Phoebe answer but she must have because he walked in the room and shut the door behind him.

I went over to the bookcase. There were so many books that I wanted to read but knew that I couldn't take many with me. I decided on three to take Tale of Two Cities, Catcher and the Rye, and The Shining. The first two I had never read and the last was an old favorite.

I raided through the cabinets and found a few boxes of some fruit bars. I added a bunch to my bag before tearing one open and eating it.

I was ready to go but it was about 30 minutes or so before Daniel and Phoebe appeared from the room. Phoebe looked a bit tired and pale.

"You ready?" she asked.

I nodded in response.

"I'm not," Daniel said.

"Hurry up. I'm ready to get out of this shit hole."

I handed a bunch of bars to Phoebe. "Put these in your bag."

She smiled, "Thank you."

I handed another handful to Daniel. He took them without looking at me. "Thanks," he said so low I barely heard him.

After a few more minutes of Daniel throwing things into his bag, we headed out. It was a very quiet journey. There were no zombies out it seemed, which would have been nice if any of us were talking but no one said a word.

Phoebe seemed to be in some kind of state of shell shock. I didn't really know why Daniel wasn't speaking. I was just much more tired than I had realized.

After a few hours of walking in weird silence and a zombie less path, we came to the point where we would part ways.

"You going to be alright? You want us to come with you? It's not too far out of the way," Phoebe suggested.

"No, you both can go to your destination, I'll be fine. Thanks though." I said.

"Okay," Phoebe said. "It's weird how much I'm going to miss you." She then gave me a long hug.

"Me too," I said into her smooth black hair.

She let go and Daniel walked up handing me a piece of paper.

"What's this?" I asked.

"It's a map, to the beach. In case things don't work out at the base. I hope they do so you can see your sister again maybe, I know how important that is. But you know, in case."

I smiled, "I thought you were mad at me earlier."

"No, just a little disappointed. I thought you might stay with us. Well, I wanted you too."

I nodded and swallowed the lump in my throat. "I'd like too but this is just something I have to do."

"I get that," he said and took me in his arms for a long embrace. I didn't want to let go. He gave me a light kiss bye. "Good luck Shelly, watch out for the dead."

"You too," I said feeling weak.

That kiss threw me under a bus. I really didn't want to part ways now. But we did. I waved to them as they set off in the other direction.

I set off towards the gates that were maybe 100 yards away or so. It didn't take long at all to get there. I couldn't believe the feeling of euphoria that filled every part of my body seeing the gates to the Navy Base. I'd made it finally. After all this time, I'd finally made it.

I walked up to the gate and was met by an annoyed guard. Before I could speak he barked, "Sorry, no access."

"I was told to come here from the Air Force base," I pulled out my I.D. to show him. "They told me you'd be sending out ships to the mainland." I finished still foolishly hopeful.

His face changed then, "When did they tell you to come?"

"Four days ago. I've had trouble getting here. My car broke down, ran into more than a few zombies, and the typhoon."

"Ma'am we had to stop sending the ships out. We couldn't risk sending out anymore."

I felt my heart drop past my intestines, past my knees and feet, and hit the ground. Deep down I knew this might happen but I had been hoping so hard.

Another guard appeared from the booth. He was a great looking black man with strong muscles and deep beautiful brown eyes.

"Unfortunately we can't let you on base," the guard in front of me said.

"What's going on?" asked the new guard.

The one I'd been talking to explained the situation. I didn't hear a word; I was drowning in my own thoughts.

"Ma'am," the new guard said to me. "I'm Calimerrio Brown, you can call me Cal. What's your name?"

He was speaking to me very softly, almost whispering.

"Shelly McCormick."

"And your husband's name was?"

"Adam," I said looking at him in confusion.

He nodded. "Jax, this is my friend Adam's wife Shelly. I went to college with Adam, roommates. Haven't seen him in ages. We've been meaning to get together since we've both been stationed here. Haven't found the time though, have we?" He looked back at me and winked.

"No," I lied feeling more confused, "it's been crazy."

"She can stay with us. You mind if I take her to my house," he stated more than asked. "I'll be back fast. I know Vanetta would love to see her. Shelly hasn't seen Nicolasa since she was a baby."

The other guard was contemplating this new information hard, "We have orders."

"Special circumstances."

Jax sighed, "Okay but your post will be an extra hour."

Cal smiled. "That's no problem. Follow me Shell."

I was confused by what had just happened but I followed Cal past the gate.

"It's not a far walk," he told me.

When we got out of earshot of Jax he said, "Hope you don't mind. Jax told me what you'd been through and I know you'd be safer here than stuck out there."

"No, thank you for sticking your neck out like that for me."

He smiled, "No problem. Not sure he completely bought it though; he's not a thick as he looks."

I giggled, "Maybe not but it still worked."

We walked for half a mile past official buildings. There was no one out. Cal told me that the base was on complete lockdown. No one was really allowed outside unless escorted by someone on duty like I was or those who were assigned to deliver rations for the week.

He told me they shut down the commissary before the national announcement so they could control the food supply. They've been delivering food to everyone on base based on how many people they have in their home. He told me the official word is they still have a few more weeks before they'll completely run out.

"They've had to keep it heavily guarded," he said, "The commissary. People have been trying to break in and steal their own food. It's just a panic reaction. I don't think any of them mean a bit of harm."

"What happens when the food runs out?" I asked

"They have a greenhouse somewhere. Growing veggies. The people delivering the food will probably be assigned hunting duties. Plus the wild chickens are great for eggs. We've managed to keep a few in our garage," he said with a smile.

He also told me the lockdown had been hard on his daughter Nicolasa known as Lasa. "She loves to play outside and since the base hasn't been affected by the outbreak, she really doesn't understand why she has to stay in."

"How old is she?"

"Five."

I nodded. It stung because Jackie came to mind. She was only a year older than this little girl. I swallowed hard and didn't say anything.

I was grateful that Cal had taken it upon himself to help me but I was thinking I probably should've stayed with Phoebe and Daniel. I was so crushed that my sister was completely snatched from me. I would never know how she was. If she made it or not. It broke my heart. All I've been through was starting to pile on me and make me feel like it would kill me before too long.

We arrived at Cal's house. "Welcome to our mansion," he joked as he opened the door.

"Daddy," I heard a little girl say as she ran to hug her father.

She was adorable with wild curly hair.

Cal picked her up into his arms and said, "Hey sweetie."

"I thought you weren't going to be home until…" a beautiful woman coming out of the kitchen had begun to say, she stopped abruptly at the sight of me. I wished once again that I had stayed with Daniel and Phoebe.

"What's going on?" she asked.

Cal put his daughter down and said, "Let me talk to you for a second. I'll be right back," he added to me before disappearing into the kitchen with his wife.

Lasa eyeballed me suspiciously.

"Hi," I said. "I'm Shelly."

I looked and saw there were coloring books on the floor.

"You want to show me what you've been coloring?"

She smiled then, "I've been doing really good. I've stayed mostly in the lines and everything. Come see." She grabbed my hand and led me to her coloring books.

I sat down on the ground next to her and she showed me the picture she'd been working on of Hello Kitty. She had other coloring books lying around. One of the Teenage Mutant Ninja Turtles that she told me a solider had brought with their food. She said she wished he had brought her something she liked more and laughed when I said there was a boy probably upset that he had a Hello Kitty coloring book.

"Well, my friend Tina would love it, she used to watch that show all the time but I can't give it to her. They won't let us leave the house," she pouted.

That's when Cal and his wife came out of the kitchen. I stood up and smiled.

"Hi Shelly," she said and extended her hand. "I'm Vanetta."

"Nice to meet you," I said and shook her hand.

Cal had to get back to his guard duty. He kissed Lasa and Vanetta bye and left.

Vanetta led me upstairs and showed me to the room I'd be staying in. It was a nice guest room with a double bed covered in a light blue comforter. I could tell Vanetta was not happy with my being there but she was trying to be pleasant. I couldn't say I blamed her, if my husband had brought some woman home out of the blue, I would've been more than a little upset myself. However, these circumstances were different. Still I understood and didn't take it personally.

I wanted to let her know the extent of my gratitude but had no idea how too.

"Thank you for doing this," I began, "letting me stay. It's..."

"Cal told me what you've been through. It's the least we could do."

"Still, thank you."

She smiled and nodded, "You're welcome."

Chapter 19

I went through my bag to get out some different clothes. When I pulled out the shirt I wanted, Jackie's stuffed animal I had tossed in the backpack fell to the ground. I hadn't thought about it since I left the house and it got shoved towards the bottom of the bag.

I picked it up off the floor and held it in my hands. I lifted the soft white cloth to my face. It smelled like Jackie, the combination of the strawberry shampoo and bubble bath that she loved. I began to cry. Much harder and more violently than I could've imagined was still in me. I realized then that I hadn't stopped to properly grieve and now I had nothing left to chase, to distract me. I was alone now with my grief.

At some point I had sat down on the bed but I didn't remember doing it. I sat there for a long time, the tears coming out of me like they'd finally burst through a dam. I couldn't stop and I grew more exhausted. I managed to change my clothes and lay down. I cried myself to sleep.

When I woke up I was a bit startled by the sight of Lasa standing over me.

"Sorry," she said when I jumped.

"It's okay. I didn't mean to fall asleep." I said and wiped my eyes as I sat up.

"What's this?" she asked picking up Jackie's toy from beside me. "You need stuffed animals to sleep too?"

"No," I began, "That belongs to my daughter Jackie."

"Oh, where is she?"

"She didn't make it sweetie."

"You mean she died like Bambi's mom?"

I nodded, "Yeah."

She looked very sad then, "I'm sorry but she went to heaven right?"

I gave a weak smile, "yeah, she went to heaven."

"This is a cool stuffed animal," she said handing it back to me. "She had good taste."

I smiled, "She did that. It was her favorite. She slept with it and took it almost everywhere."

"How old was she?"

"Six."

"I'm almost six; I'll be six next month."

"Really? She turned six two months ago. She would've liked you I think."

"What was her name?"

"Jackie."

I hadn't really talked about Jackie to this length before. I don't know what it was about this sweet little girl that made me open up. Or maybe it was just time to open up about her. I'd talked to Daniel and Phoebe briefly but I wanted to seem so strong that I didn't let myself come undone. The façade was over now, I couldn't hold on to that illusion of strength anymore.

"You want to watch over it for me?" I asked handing her the little stuffed animal.

"Me?"

"Yeah, I think Jackie would like to know someone is appreciating it like she would have."

She had a big smile on her face, "Thanks, I'll take really good care of it, I promise."

She turned around and ran out of the room going, "Mom!"

I sat alone in the room for a few minutes still feeling completely exhausted. I took a deep breath and grabbed the last bottle of water I had in my bag. I took a long refreshing sip.

I got up and walked into the hall. Vanetta was just coming out of her room. Lasa ran past her and bound down the stairs.

"I overheard you talking to Lasa," she said wrapping her arms around her waist. "I'm really sorry about your daughter."

"Thank you," I said quietly.

She then took me into a strong embrace, taking me completely off guard. I hugged her back after recovering from the shock of it.

She let go and walked down the hallway to the stairs.

"Honestly, I was a little pissed when Cal brought you home."

I laughed, "I completely understand. I wouldn't have liked it much either."

"Cal's got such a big heart. Helps where he thinks it's needed. And I'm still not used to this new situation we find ourselves in."

"Me either."

She nodded, "you want to help me fix dinner?"

"Least I could do for you putting a roof over my head."

She laughed and I followed her down the stairs. Vanetta made stuffed peppers with ground chicken and taco seasoning. She said something about having to get creative with her meals since the rations. The stove still worked since it was a gas stove.

I made a salad and buttered the bread to be toasted. It wasn't much but it helped to just be moving and doing something.

We talked a bit. I told her about Adam and that whole situation. She had a butcher knife in her hand and demonstrated on a carrot how she would've taken care of him. I began to laugh extremely hard. It was the hardest I'd laughed since all this shit began.

We ate when Cal got home by candle and lantern light. It was a delicious meal. Vanetta was an amazing cook. Lasa complimented me on the salad. It was adorable of her.

It was lovely to be with this family but I found myself worried and wondering about Daniel and Phoebe. I missed them terribly. It was amazing really how attached I'd become to them. They had become like a family to me and helped me survive.

After dinner, I went to bed. Since the dam broke inside me I was nothing but tired.

It wasn't very long before I felt someone shaking me and I opened my eyes.

"Shelly," Lasa said. "Would you like some company? I don't really like sleeping by myself but I know I bother my dad and he's got to get up early."

I smiled, "sure sweetie. You can sleep in here."

She crawled in the other side of the bed.

"Shelly, can you tell me a story?"

"Sure," I said.

I always made up stories for Jackie to get her to sleep. Mostly because I could never remember all of what happened in a story or I confused one story with another.

"What kind of story?"

"A princess story."

"Alright, once upon a time there was a beautiful princess who longed to leave her palace walls. But her father, the King, was fearful that she would be in danger if ever she left. Tired of always being stuck on the grounds of the castle she decided she would run away. She snuck out during the night and got on her horse. She rode for a long time and ended up far away. It was the dead of winter and the princess hadn't thought about how cold it would be. It was dark and..."

I heard the heavy breathing, the sound of a child deep and fast asleep.

I smiled, "she realized that the most important place to be was home. She made it back safely and though she would leave from time to time, she would never forget how wonderful it was to be safe at home."

I closed my eyes and drifted off to sleep. My dream took me to the house I grew up in in Michigan but it was nicer with a white picket fence. My parents sat at a picnic table laughing at something my sister Cate had just said. I brought out a pitcher of lemonade while my husband Daniel was grilling up some food. Our two girls Jackie and Lasa ran around the backyard playing and laughing.

I woke up crying silently and extremely confused. The happy dreams weren't any better than the nightmares.

Chapter 20

The weeks passed slowly but surely. I did my best to help out around the house. I played with Lasa and we colored. I cooked with Vanetta and collected the eggs from the chickens in the garage. I was passing the time but I felt more like a zombie than the reanimated corpses that were roaming the island. My mission had failed and without the goal of trying to get to my sister, as doomed as it was, without it I was empty. I had nothing left.

Though I loved this beautiful family that had taken me in, I didn't feel like I belonged. I felt like a burden on them though they never acted like I was. I felt odd and out of place most of the time. I tried to help and keep out of the way.

A bright spot was Lasa. I felt a real kinship with her. She reminded me of Jackie so much in the way she laughed and carried herself. Even some of the things she said sounded like they could've easily been quotes she stole from Jackie. It hurt like hell to be around this precious little girl that reminded me so much of the precious one I lost but at the same time it was like a blessing to feel close to Jackie in a way.

Lasa slept with me every night after that first night. The dreams I'd been having become less frequent and I was having almost good nights of sleep. Lasa was becoming more of a comforting presence to me than I believe I was to her. Perhaps part of it was being safe away from those awful creatures. The threat didn't seem to exist in the shelter of this home.

Vanetta was appreciative of the fact I let Lasa stay in the room with me. Cal had been working 12 hour posts since this whole thing started. It made sense, we were at war.

Cal was upbeat and sweet but Lasa kept him awake when she came in the room with them. I could understand why, she liked to snuggle up close and didn't leave a lot of room to adjust. But that was another thing that reminded me so much of Jackie. Where it kept Cal awake, it helped me rest.

It was nice to be part of something that felt so normal after all the chaos. Though, it was hard for me to appreciate it all. I was just waiting for the other shoe to drop.

I became ill the third week I had been there. It was nothing too major but I was nauseous all the time and couldn't keep much down. Which was sort of a blessing, since food supplies were due to run out any day.

Vanetta made me a tea remedy that helped with the nausea that her mother had passed down to her. It helped but I still didn't feel like eating much.

I liked Vanetta a lot. I felt we would've been friends in real life before the dead began to walk the earth. She was funny and tough. I loved talking with her. She told me about growing up in Mississippi. Her and Cal met in the sweetest way. They met while working at Disney World together doing some kind of work program they had for college kids. I'd never even heard of it but it sounded like something Jackie would've loved to do had she been able to grow up.

Little things reminded me of Jackie everyday. Though I missed her terribly all the time, I was getting better at living with the constant ache in my heart.

After a wonderful month of a normal life, things turned. Lasa and I were sitting at the table coloring books when the sirens went off, warning that something had gone wrong.

Vanetta came into the room. Her face was the picture of panic. She was almost hyperventilating.

"Upstairs Lasa," she said.

"But mom."

"Now!" Vanetta commanded.

Lasa was pouting but did as her mother said. When she was no longer in the room, I spoke.

"What is it?"

"They said they would only put on the sirens if security was breached by those things. Cal's at the post."

"He'll be alright." I said though I had a sickening feeling in the pit of my stomach.

I made Vanetta some tea to calm her nerves. She sat at the table biting her nails. It was hard to see this pillar of strength so scared. It unnerved me.

I handed her the tea and told her I would check on Lasa. The siren hadn't stopped yet.

I went up the stairs to Lasa's room but she wasn't there. I walked out and looked down the hall to see her in the guest room. She was holding Jackie's stuffed animal while she sat on the bed.

"Hey," I said. "You okay?"

She nodded then shrugged, "yeah sort of. I'm just scared."

"Me too sweetie."

She looked at me, "adults shouldn't tell kids they're scared. It makes them more scared."

I laughed and walked in the room, taking a seat next to her.

"But it's okay to be scared. Just because we're both scared isn't a bad thing, it just means we have to be brave."

"Brave?"

"Yeah, being scared isn't bad; it's how you handle being scared. Right now, what we have to do is be brave."

She nodded, "I can be brave."

"I know you can."

I heard the front door open and it took a minute or two before it shut. Then I heard a loud ear piercing scream. It was a scream that I had heard before in recent memory and the result was not good.

I had grabbed my gun from its hiding place just in case.

Lasa had terror in her eyes now. I told her to stay put. I went out of the room and shut the door behind me.

I walked cautiously down the stairs. I saw no sign of anyone in the front room. I continued on into the kitchen slowly. That's where I found them.

A reanimated Cal sat lifeless against the cabinets. He had black liquid coming out of the side of his head, where he had been stabbed.

I looked and my heart broke when I saw Vanetta. She was sitting against the opposite cabinet and the bloody knife in hand. It wasn't easy to miss the bite mark on her shoulder. There was a huge chunk of skin missing and blood was pouring out of the wound.

I put my gun down and walked over to her. I knelt by her side.

She smiled weakly, "how long do I have?"

"I don't know. I've never seen anyone change."

She closed her eyes. Tears crept down her face.

"You have to go," she said.

"I can't leave you like this," I protested.

"Shelly, what good will staying do? You can't help or change what's going to happen."

I knew that she was right but I felt awful. I was just going to leave her to die all alone.

"Take care of Lasa. She'll be in good hands with you."

"I will," I said fighting back the tears.

She touched my face lightly, "thank you."

I took her hand and kissed it, "bye."

Her eyes shut then. She was gone and it wouldn't be long before she turned into one of those things. I took the knife with the blood and put it through the side of her head.

I dropped the knife on the floor and began to cry harder. I didn't indulge myself for long. I needed to get Lasa out of there.

I wiped my tears and grabbed my gun off the counter.

I went back upstairs to the room. Lasa was still on the bed squeezing the stuffed animal.

Cal and Vanetta had said they kept bags ready to go just in case in their closet. They had mentioned that there was one for Lasa in there as well, so I knew at least I didn't have to pack.

"Lasa, sweetie. We need to leave," I stated calmly.

She looked at me, tears in her big brown eyes.

"Where are mommy and daddy?"

"They can't come with us," I said.

"Are they like Bambi's mom?" she asked.

I nodded. "They're like Bambi's mom."

She buried her face into the stuffed animal and held it tighter.

"I really hate that movie," she stated.

"I'm sorry sweetie but we need to go."

I grabbed my stuff and got Lasa's out of the closet. We walked down the stairs together. I didn't let go of her hand. I didn't want her to go in the kitchen and see her parents. She was too young.

I grabbed their keys from the hook by the front door. I opened the door to see zombies making their way down the street.

Lasa opened her mouth to scream but I managed to cover her mouth with my hand before a peep came out.

"Lasa the main thing right now is not bringing attention to ourselves. We've got to try to get to the Jeep as quietly as possible. Okay?"

Her eyes were about twice their normal size but she nodded.

"Alright, let's go."

I went out the door with Lasa behind me. We walked slowly to the Jeep which was 10 feet away. It felt like it took an eternity to get to it. The zombies kept walking forward without looking our direction.

I opened the door for Lasa to get in. I put our bags in next to her and shut the door as quietly as I could.

We almost made it but I dropped the keys. I picked them up quickly but I hit the little red button as grabbed them.

The horn screamed into the air, asking, begging to be listened to. The panic button had caused a new panic in me.

I hit the button to cut it off but the three seconds it was going off was all it took.

The zombies had turned their attention to the Jeep and where I stood. They were moving slowly but fast enough to be a problem.

I opened the front door and hopped in. I locked the doors. I dropped the keys on the floor trying to get them in the ignition.

I knew I needed to calm down. I took a deep breath and grabbed the keys. I managed to get the car started this time.

Lasa was sitting in the floor board between the seats. Her eyes were shut tight and she was squeezing the stuffed animal.

All I saw in the rearview were dead faces coming at us. They were coming towards the driver side of the car as well. The only clear path was to the right.

There was an empty field there and just across it, the road was clear.

I thanked God we were in a Jeep. I turned the wheel hard and drove fast through the field.

I saw the zombies in the rearview try and turn their bodies quickly in the new direction of their food. Some of them fell trying to turn that quickly.

I managed to put a good amount of distance between the Jeep and the herd.

I got onto the road which wasn't as clear as it had appeared at first. Still with a little bit of daylight left, I didn't have to turn on the headlights and that saved a bit of notice.

I managed to get to the gate without too much difficulty. There was no one there now. There were a few dead bodies as we exited the base. There were also body parts strewn about and zombies feeding on the bodies. I felt even sicker than I had been the last few days but ignored the chunk rising in my throat.

We had to find a place before night fall. That was the mission. The further we got from the base, the less dense the herd of zombies had become. After a while, I managed to find a good area with a few trees to pull over at. There were no zombies around.

Lasa was still in the floorboard with her eyes shut tight. Tears were streaming down her face.

"Lasa," I said gently.

She looked at me and sniffled, "I want my mom."

I touched the top of her head, "I know sweetie, I'm sorry."

"Are we staying here?"

"For the night. We'll move on in the morning."

She nodded and said nothing more. Poor child had lost her whole world. We were in a similar boat but I wasn't the five year old whose world had been pulled out from under her. I hoped I could take care of her. Maybe we'd help heal each other. It was a long shot dream but if nothing else maybe we'd be a comfort to each other in this mess.

I got her Jackie's blanket I'd taken from my car and wrapped her up in it. I was surprised by how quickly she fell asleep.

I didn't sleep at all. I had to protect Lasa from any zombies. I didn't even feel tired because for the first time in a month I felt like I had a purpose. I wasn't just surviving.

Epilogue

The time passed slowly that night. My senses were heightened and I felt electric and alive. I felt alive for the first time in a very long time.

No zombies came near the vehicle during the night. I couldn't even hear them in the distance which felt strange and made me paranoid.

Lasa woke up shortly after the sun came up. She yawned and stretched her arms. It was a few moments before the reality set in. I could tell by the way her face changed.

"Morning," I said softly. "You hungry?"

She nodded. "And I really need to pee."

I got my gun and got out of the car. I led her to an area where there were a few bushes. I made sure the area was secure before she did her business. After she was done, we walked back to the Jeep.

"So what happens now?" she asked.

I shrugged, "I don't know. Let's just worry about breakfast right now."

We both climbed back into the back seat. I gave Lasa some hand sanitizer. I dug in my bag for the breakfast bars I had taken before leaving the other house. I hadn't touched any of them. Staying with the Browns meant I had plenty of food to eat so I left them in my bag just in case. I was glad I did.

I handed a bar to Lasa.

"Apple, I love the apple ones." She said and peeled off the wrapper.

I dug my hand in again to get one for myself and instead grabbed a piece of paper. I took it out to look at it. It had a badly drawn map on it. Though it was terribly drawn I knew what it was and I could follow it.

I smiled when I saw it.

"What?" Lasa asked.

I shook my head a little, "I just came up with a place for us to go."

"Is it safe?"

I wasn't sure how to answer that truly. We should've been safe where we had been. I didn't know if safe was an option in this world.

"I think we'll be safe."

She nodded, "if that's the best you can do."

I laughed a little. I ate my breakfast bar. We both drank a little bit of water.

I climbed over the seat into the front.

"You ready?" I asked.

Lasa nodded, "yeah. Do you think I'll like it there?"

I looked at Lasa's face in the rearview, "I think we'll both like it there."

I kicked the engine into life and put her in gear. I turned around and headed west following Daniel's map.

I was feeling hopeful that we were headed to someplace we could call home. I had watched so much loss, so much death. It would be foolish to believe that there would be none in the future. Yet, I had hope. That Cate was alive somewhere in Arizona, that Daniel and I would maybe be able to start something worth fighting for, and that Lasa would have a future of more than just zombie attacks and heartache. I hoped that life would endure the plague of the dead, that we would all find a way to rebuild.

Printed in Great Britain
by Amazon